VISION.

The backdrop of the stadium flips ⸺ ⸺ *disappear.*
The track morphs into a rain-slick ⸺ ⸺ *ne,*
a random jumble of numbers dri ⸺ ⸺ *og.*
Twin headlights cut through the da ⸺ ⸺ *y to*
scream, but I can't make a sound.

"Ashlyn!"

In one blink, the stadium swirled back into place. I swayed a little and had to take a step to keep my balance.

"Are you okay?" Coach Roberts was staring at me like I had a third eye. "You look kind of pale."

I started to give her the automatic "I'm fine," but I wasn't. Not by a long shot. "I . . . I'm just . . ." I glanced down at the score sheet in my hand and my knees felt weak. Bold, black numbers sprawled across the paper. Ice settled in the pit of my stomach. How could it be happening again? The trances had never come so close together before. "I think I need to sit down."

It didn't make sense. Not only had I been pulled into another trance, but the images were a repeat of what I had seen the day before. A repeat of an accident scene I knew too well.

The wet road. Bright lights stabbing my eyes.

It couldn't be. Kyra and I had never seen the same vision twice. It was like I was seeing my own accident. . . .

I didn't want to follow that thought. If I was just now seeing the images I should have seen before the accident, what did it mean? Would all the trances I had missed for the past several weeks come back to haunt me?

Or just the one that killed my mom?

TRANCE

LINDA GERBER

speak

An Imprint of Penguin Group (USA) Inc.

SPEAK
Published by the Penguin Group
Penguin Group (USA) Inc., 345 Hudson Street, New York, New York 10014, U.S.A.
Penguin Group (Canada), 90 Eglinton Avenue East, Suite 700, Toronto, Ontario, Canada M4P 2Y3
(a division of Pearson Penguin Canada Inc.)
Penguin Books Ltd, 80 Strand, London WC2R 0RL, England
Penguin Ireland, 25 St Stephen's Green, Dublin 2, Ireland (a division of Penguin Books Ltd)
Penguin Group (Australia), 250 Camberwell Road, Camberwell, Victoria 3124, Australia
(a division of Pearson Australia Group Pty Ltd)
Penguin Books India Pvt Ltd, 11 Community Centre, Panchsheel Park, New Delhi - 110 017, India
Penguin Group (NZ), 67 Apollo Drive, Rosedale, North Shore 0632, New Zealand
(a division of Pearson New Zealand Ltd)
Penguin Books (South Africa) (Pty) Ltd, 24 Sturdee Avenue,
Rosebank, Johannesburg 2196, South Africa

Registered Offices: Penguin Books Ltd, 80 Strand, London WC2R 0RL, England

Published by Speak, an imprint of Penguin Group (USA) Inc., 2010

1 3 5 7 9 10 8 6 4 2

LIBRARY OF CONGRESS CATALOG-IN-PUBLICATION DATA
Gerber, Linda C.
Trance / by Linda Gerber.
p. cm.
Summary: Ashlyn was unable to use her visions of the future to save her mother's life,
but as she begins to understand and control them somewhat, she realizes
that love interest Jake is the subject of her most recent trances.
ISBN: 978-0-14-241415-6
[1. Extrasensory perception—Fiction. 2. Grief—Fiction. 3. Traffic accidents—Fiction.
4. Fathers and daughters—Fiction. 5. High schools—Fiction. 6. Schools—Fiction.]
I. Title
PZ7.G293567Tr 2010
[Fic]—dc22 2009052872

Speak ISBN 978-0-14-241415-6

Printed in the United States of America

To Sandra, Tricia, and Donna

for showing how strong the bonds of sisters can be.

ACKNOWLEDGMENTS

As always, I am humbled and very grateful for the efforts of so many who helped to bring this book about. Huge thanks to my agent, Elaine Spencer, for making it all happen. This is our first baby together. Elaine we did it! And to my very patient editor, Angelle Pilkington, who continues to guide and encourage me no matter how dim I can be. Thank you, Angelle! Special thanks to Adrianne Mecham for explaining the power of numbers. Aaron, Clark, Jenna, Haley, and Dalan, you are my rocks. Karen, Kate, Marsha, Jen, Ginger, Nicole, Julie, and Barb, you keep me going. Lisa and Becca, thanks for reading! And finally, the book wouldn't look so pretty without the genius of Theresa Evangelista. Thank you!

PROLOGUE

Sounds are what I remember most. The crunch of metal on metal. Shattering glass. Screams. The wail of the ambulance siren.

I woke to new sounds in the hospital. The steady drip of an IV bag. The rhythmic beep of a heart monitor. The soft crying of my dad and my sister as they huddled in separate corners of the room.

On the day of the funeral, the sounds were muted, muffled as if draped under a shroud. Friends and neighbors, all in black, murmured condolences as they shuffled past my wheelchair. The bishop's voice droned into white noise as he prayed a final blessing. The wheels on the pulleys squeaked, lowering my mom's coffin into the grave.

At home there were no sounds, only silence.

Nothing to fill the empty spaces.

Nothing to buffer me from my guilt.

Nothing to stand in the way of the trances.

"**A**re you sure you're up to this?" Michelle flicked the blinker and glanced over her shoulder to change lanes. "If it's too soon . . ."

"It's fine," I said for about the eight hundredth time that day. "Or at least it will be if you quit asking about it."

She shot me a look over the top of her Ray-Bans and made a big show of pressing her lips together.

I sighed and picked at the stitching on my backpack. Michelle was just worrying, because that's what best friends do. So I apologized—because backing down is what I do. "I'm sorry, Shel. I have to do this, though; I need the job. No one else is going to work around our meets the way Carole does."

"Right." Michelle drummed her fingers on the steering wheel. "If she's so understanding, why is she making you transfer to Westland Mall?"

"She's not *making* me do anything. She had to fill my position at Polaris Mall while I was gone and this one opened up." I was beginning to regret asking Michelle for a ride after track practice. "Can we drop this, please?"

She pressed her lips together again—tight, like it was killing her to keep the words inside—and stared straight ahead.

I sighed and went back to picking at my backpack. To be fair, I understood why Michelle was acting so uptight. The last time I had been to the Westland Mall was the day of the accident. My mom had insisted on riding along with me since I'd only had my license about three weeks. We were on our way home when we got hit.

If Michelle thought returning to Westland would be hard for me because it would bring back memories of that day, she was only half right. Michelle understands a lot about me, but not everything. Not that. There are things I can't tell even her. Like how I should have seen the accident coming. How I should have tried to stop it. How if it wasn't for me, my mom might still be alive.

My sister, Kyra, and I see things before they happen. Not entire events—snapshots, like pieces of a puzzle. Kyra sees some of the pieces and I see the others. If we're lucky, we can fit the puzzle together and guess what's coming.

On the day of the accident, Kyra knew something bad

was going to happen. She tried to warn me, but I wouldn't listen. I didn't even try. That's the part that haunts me most.

Michelle swatted my arm. "Did you even hear what I said?"

I blinked back to the present. "I'm sorry. What?"

She lowered her dark glasses and gestured out my window with her eyes. "Check it out. Two o'clock."

I followed her gaze. On a motorcycle in the lane next to us was a guy who, I will admit, was not at all hard to look at. I couldn't really see his face because it was obscured by aviator sunglasses and a scuffed black helmet, but I was pretty sure it wasn't his face Michelle was interested in. She was probably much more taken by the athlete's build beneath his T-shirt and jeans. Impressively contoured, his muscles tensed as he leaned forward, gripping the handlebars.

Michelle sighed dramatically and I raised my brows at her. "I thought you only had eyes for Trey." Trey was one of the guys from the track team. He and Michelle were, as she emphatically put it, "just friends," but I knew she wanted more.

"Nothing wrong with appreciating a fine work of art," she said.

The artwork in question pulled ahead and signaled with one well-toned arm to change lanes, so that he was riding directly in front of us.

"Oh. My." Michelle fanned her face with her hand. "I've died and gone to heaven."

I actually might have laughed at that if Michelle hadn't suddenly realized what she'd said. Her face went white and she clapped a hand over her mouth. "Oh, Lynnie, I'm so sorry. I didn't mean to—"

"Don't worry about it."

"I wasn't even thinking."

"Really. It's fine." I focused on our motorcycle guy, watching the muscles play across his back as he slowed and signaled again to make the turn into the mall parking lot.

The mall. My stomach folded in on itself. No matter what I said to Michelle, I wasn't sure I was ready for it. But then, I didn't have a choice.

Motorcycle Guy began his turn across traffic and Michelle blindly followed like she was connected to his rear-wheel fender. She must have been watching him instead of the road because she didn't seem to be aware of the car in the oncoming lane, headed straight for us. I stomped both feet against the floor and reached out to brace myself for the impact.

The car was almost on top of us before I could find my voice. "Look out!"

Michelle slammed on the brakes. Her tires screeched as they dug into the pavement. My seat belt locked tight, tethering me to the seat, but Michelle's purse flew forward and slammed into the dashboard. Her stuff rained down all over the floor mats.

"Idiot!" she yelled.

I stared at the road, heart hammering against my ribs so hard I thought it was going to break through. My chest felt hot and tight. I couldn't breathe. In my head, I heard the echo of another screech of brakes. Felt the impact. Tasted the salted copper tang of blood in my mouth.

Michelle's hands tightened around the steering wheel like she wanted to fold it in two. She managed to guide the car into the parking lot. "What a jerk!" she raged. "Did you see how fast he was going?"

Even if I'd wanted to answer her, I couldn't have. My throat felt like a clenched fist. I avoided her eyes and reached down to grab her cell phone from the floor. Fished her wallet from under my seat. Grabbed a coral pink tube of lip gloss. My hands were shaking so badly I had to try twice before I was able to stuff everything back into her purse.

By the time I sat up again, Michelle had gotten really quiet. "I'm so sorry, Lynnie. I wasn't paying attention. I should have—"

"It's okay," I said, as much to myself as to her. "No one's hurt."

"You want me to take you home?" Her voice had gone soft. Apologetic. "You could call in sick to work."

"What are you talking about?" I set her purse back on

the console and fussed with it until the handles rested against each other just so. "I'm fine."

She frowned, unconvinced. "Look, if you need anything . . ."

Suddenly, the car felt very small. Airless. I had to get out so I could breathe. I grabbed my backpack. "Stop here," I said. "I can cut through Nordstrom." I had the door half open before she had even pulled up to the curb, and jumped out the moment she stopped. "Thanks for the ride."

"Lynnie . . ." She leaned across the passenger seat, looking up at me with that same concerned, pitying look on her face. I closed the door and stepped back before she could say anything more.

It had been eight weeks since the accident. Eight weeks, three days, and twenty-one hours. Most of that time was spent in the hospital and then in rehab, trying to get my legs to function the way they used to. If I worked at it hard enough, the doctors said, I could run again. At least that was one thing I was able to get back.

My physical therapist said she had never seen someone go at the exercises the way I did. She thought it meant I was brave, but really, it was an escape. The therapy gave me a place to push the pain. It gave me something to concentrate on instead of the guilt.

As soon as Michelle signaled and pulled out into the parking lot, I turned and ran for the Nordstrom entrance. *I shouldn't have cut her off*, I thought. She was just worried; that shouldn't annoy me. Since I couldn't bring myself to drive since the accident, I should be glad she was so willing to give me rides. When I got to work I should call her and—

I was almost to the door when a guy ran past me, bumping my arm. He was smoothing down a shock of brown hair with one hand and poking at the tails of a white dress shirt with the other, trying, I guessed, to tuck it into the waistband of his rumpled jeans. A gag-worthy bright colored tie with music notes all over it swung like a noose around his neck.

"Sorry!" he called over his shoulder.

"It's okay," I called back.

He pulled the door open, but instead of rushing through it like I expected him to, he stopped, buttoning the collar of his shirt as he held the door open with his foot.

For me, I realized.

Heat flooded my face as I slipped past him into the breezeway. "Thanks," I murmured.

"No problem." He let the outside door go and then hurried to open the interior door, again waiting as he held it open for me.

I thanked him once more and glanced up just long enough to meet his smiling green eyes, then quickly looked away as my face felt like it was going to combust.

"Have a good one," he said, and took off again.

"Yeah," I called after him. *Yeah?* That's all I could come up with? I felt so stupid that I hung back and let him get well ahead of me before following him through Nordstrom toward the mall's center court.

Being at Westland Mall again was like wandering through some kind of dreamscape—familiar and strange at the same time. Michelle and I used to come to this mall all the time, but now I felt like an intruder, out of place and conspicuous.

The feeling only intensified when I spotted the ShutterBugz kiosk on the other side of the mall's center court. Behind the counter, a very pregnant clerk perched on the stool, absently twirling her black hair as she flipped through the pages of a magazine. Large silver hoops hung from her ears, and on her wrists a collection of metallic bracelets jangled every time she moved. With her heavy eyeliner and bloodred lips, she could almost pass for a Gypsy—if it wasn't for the ShutterBugz apron stretching tight across her stomach.

She glanced up as I got closer and gave me the kind of once-over a girl might give to her boyfriend's ex. Only that wasn't likely since she looked like she was at least ten years older than I was. "Ashlyn Greenfield?"

"That's me."

"You're late." She slapped her magazine shut and eased off of the stool—carefully, like she had to balance the load in front of her.

I started to apologize, but she held up her hand to stop me. "Whatever. I've got to pee." She untied the strings of her apron. "Well, come on. I can't wait all night."

I squeezed in beside her to take my place behind the counter and she looked me up and down again. "You know how to close out the register?" she asked.

I nodded. "Yeah. No worries."

"Good." She pushed the apron at me and stuffed her magazine into an oversized leather bag, all in one motion. "Keys are in the side drawer," she said, zipping the bag closed.

With one last appraising look, she slung the straps of her bag onto her shoulder and waddled out of the kiosk toward the food court. I knew from when I used to hang out at Westland that was where the closest restroom could be found.

I watched her go until she disappeared behind the rows of tables and then I pulled the loop of the apron over my head. As I tied the strings in back, I turned in a slow circle, checking out my new surroundings. No, that's wrong. The surroundings weren't new; nothing in the mall had changed. It was me. I felt like I was in one of those forgetting dreams, but instead of wandering down the main hallway at school in nothing but my underwear, I was standing behind the counter of a kiosk I barely even noticed before the accident. And I felt lost.

That's when I saw the guy with the tie who had opened

the door for me earlier. He was adjusting the height of a stool next to the grand piano displayed in Kinnear Music's huge front window. He must work there, I realized. Suddenly, the tie made sense.

Now, with the safety of distance between us, I was able to get a better look at him. He had dark hair and dark eyes—green, I remembered, and then was surprised by the recollection. The planes of his face were angular, but just soft enough that he looked like he could be about my age. I hadn't seen him around school, so maybe he went to Mountain View or East. I wondered absently if I might bump into him at one of our track meets. He did have an athletic build. Maybe a little thick through the shoulders to be a sprinter, but he could do shot put, or even javelin.

But then, he wasn't dressed like a jock. I'm not exactly sure *what* he was dressed like. From the waist up, he was all buttoned up and mall-ified in his white shirt and tie, the perfect music-store employee. But from the waist down, he was someone else altogether in worn jeans and scuffed black motorcycle boots.

He sat at the piano, hands hovering over the keys for an instant before he began to play. The first angry chords took me by surprise but then I was caught by the energy of the piece and I couldn't look away. It was like a dance the way his whole body moved to make each note. I didn't even know what song it was, but I knew he commanded it, moved it, made it come alive.

But then some gray-haired guy in a stuffy blue suit and the same tacky music-note tie steamed up to the display area, gesturing wildly with his hands. Tie Guy stopped playing and Gray Hair turned on his heel, marching to the back of the store. I could almost hear the sigh as the tie guy's shoulders rose and then deflated. He now stared at the piano as if it were an open trap, waiting to snare him. When he started to play again—some lame tune I'd probably heard in an elevator somewhere—the life had bled from his music.

In that instant I felt a kind of kinship with the ugly tie guy. I knew what it was like to be so close to something real and not be able to touch it. I knew what it was like to be someone you're not.

M y dad thought going back to work at "the photography studio" would be good for me, a healing step toward something I had loved. He actually told me that, as if he had any idea.

ShutterBugz was no studio. It consisted of a backdrop wall, a sad collection of stools, tables, drapes and props, a camera mounted on a stationary tripod, and a couple of light umbrellas. Everything was automated—the lighting, the angles, the aperture, the focus. "Not art photography," as Carole would say, "but what can you expect for nine ninety-nine?"

What Dad didn't get was that working at ShutterBugz was no step toward anything I loved; it was insulation against it. Even before the accident, I used my job there as a retreat. I didn't have to think. I didn't have to feel. Real photography is raw and honest. Kiosk pictures are plastic and fake. That was what I wanted. I didn't do real anymore. Real hurt too much.

That's why when Carole asked if I could take the open spot at Westland Mall, I said yes. Westland was no place I wanted to be, but it was better than sitting alone in my empty house, remembering everything I had done wrong to get me to that place.

Not that work was providing much of a distraction. I only had three customers the entire evening—one couple who pretty much wanted me to document their make-out session, one totally adorable baby, and possibly the brattiest three-year-old I have ever met.

I'm serious. This kid—Evan was his name—pouted, screamed, threw the props, hit his mother and probably would have hit me too, if I'd have let him get close enough. The mom wasn't helping, either. The more Evan pouted, the more uptight she got until you could see the veins in her neck sticking out and her face took on an unnatural shade of puce.

"Smile for Mama," she demanded. "Be good. Sit still for the nice lady or you will lose your TV time, Evan."

I finally had to make the mom wait on the other side of the partition. Parents don't get that they really are not helping sometimes.

I pulled out the entire arsenal to deal with this kid, from the ShutterBugz hand puppet—a psychedelic beetle in metallic purples and pinks—to the ShutterBugz antennae—a headband that I stuck on my head, featuring two purple glittered Ping-Pong balls atop bouncy springs.

With the camera remote in one hand and the puppet in the other, I hopped up and down in front of Evan, dancing like a fool. "Hey, Evan! Look!" I fluttered the puppet bug up over my head and then zoomed it down toward him.

He shrieked. And it wasn't the nice little-kid-laughing kind of shriek, either. Clearly, he was not a fan of the hand puppet. I threw it aside and shook my head so that the glitter balls wobbled. "Look here, Evan," I sang. "Right up here. Let's get a nice smile. Come on."

More shrieking. I wanted to strangle the little monster. And then suddenly from behind me came a terrible noise. "Yaaaaaaah!"

Evan stopped shrieking and blinked his big eyes in surprise. His lips curled up in what could possibly pass as a smile before he let loose again with a bloodcurdling yowl. But that was enough. I had managed to snap a shot in his moment of silence and turned to see what had caused the distraction.

Tie Guy grinned and tipped his head to me.

"Thank you," I mouthed.

He nodded and went back to work.

Evan's mom was happy enough with the photo that she ordered a complete package. That, or she was so mortified by her son's behavior that she just wanted to escape from the mall. Either one was fine by me.

I was just finishing up with the order forms when I heard Nick Cumberland's voice. I knew it was him without looking, but I couldn't help myself. It's like my eyes were caught in some kind of tractor beam that forced them up, up until I had visual confirmation.

Sure enough, Nick was strolling through the center court with a bunch of his football buddies. They were all laughing about something and punching each other and talking way too loud.

My heart dropped as if someone had thrown it from a tall building. This was part of the reason I had hesitated about transferring to Westland Mall. People I knew hung out here. People like Nick.

Getting mixed up with Nick Cumberland was one of the many mistakes I made before the accident. I'd been careful to stay away from him ever since—skipping out of the class we shared before the bell rang and avoiding the jock hangout in B wing even if that meant walking outside in the rain to reach my locker in C wing.

But there was nothing I could do now, stuck behind the ShutterBugz counter. I stood there helplessly and could only watch as Nick and his friends wandered closer. He glanced up and I didn't look away quickly enough and our eyes met—only for a moment, but long enough for an ice blue jolt to shoot straight through me. I quickly bent over the order forms and tried to pretend not to know he was there.

"Hey! Greenfield!" he said. "Is that you?"

By then he was standing right in front of the kiosk and it was impossible to ignore him. That didn't mean I had to look at him, though.

"Hey, I didn't know you worked here," he said.

My face felt tight as I forced it into a smile. "I just started," I said, concentrating on the fuzzy *S* of his letter jacket.

"Nice bobbles."

"Ex*cuse* me?"

He gestured to my head.

"Oh." I yanked off the headband. "They're antennae."

"Of course they are."

We stood there, awkwardly fidgeting for a moment, and then he leaned toward me, resting his hands on the narrow counter between us. "How've you been?"

I bunched my shoulders. "Good. You?"

"Good."

"That's . . . great. I'm, uh . . ." I gestured toward the back of the kiosk. "I've got to straighten up the photo area . . ."

"Wait. Ashlyn, look at me."

His voice froze me where I stood. I could feel each second ticking away until finally—against my better judgment—I let my gaze go to him again and still, after all that had happened, my stomach flipped. I don't know if it was the way his soft brown eyes held mine, or the sadness in his smile, or the way his hair curled up just a bit at the edge of his collar. He made me weak.

"I've been thinking about you." Nick reached for my hand and instinctively I jerked it away. His smile faded and he managed to look wounded. "Come on, Greenfield." His voice was soft and pleading. "Don't do that. I'm trying to make nice."

"You don't have to—"

"Look, I feel bad about what happened," he said. "Really bad. I should have been there for you. I feel like the whole thing was my fault."

I didn't want to hear the rest, but I couldn't help myself. "The whole thing?"

He shuffled a little and looked down at his feet. "You know, you and me. That day . . ." Behind him, his friends stood watching us as if we were a play-off game in double overtime. He glanced back at them and then lowered his voice. "Look. I don't want to do this here. What time do you get off work? Maybe we could go someplace quiet . . ."

Not long ago I would have given anything to go off "someplace quiet" with Nick Cumberland. I'd had a thing for the guy since seventh grade. But things change. "I don't think so."

"Come on, Greenfield. I'm trying." He reached across the counter and made another grab for my hand, successfully this time, and pulled me toward him so all that stood between us was the narrow strip of counter. "I know I should have tried to talk to you before," he said, "I just didn't know what to say. But I'm here now. The least you could do is listen to me."

Once again I felt myself drawn to Nick's velvet brown eyes. Those eyes used to have the power to make me melt like a Popsicle in July. And as close as we stood, his spicy, outdoorsy guy smell surrounded me, just the way I remembered. It made my knees tremble, which is probably the effect he was going for. I pulled away. "I'm sorry, Nick. I have to get back to work."

His lips tightened and whatever softness I thought I had seen before disappeared. He dropped my hand. "Yeah. You do that."

I sat heavily on the stool and watched him go. Relieved. Hurt. Humiliated.

And then, without warning, it hit me. A hot buzzing filled my head and darkness immediately closed in on my vision. I could see my hand reaching for the pencil. Feel the way my face went dead. Hear the lead *scritch, scritch, scritch* across the paper.

The last thing I remembered before it all went black was the time on my watch.

8:22.

I'm standing in the dark. Hot pink numbers form in the air above me. I reach for them but before my fingers can touch them, they dissolve, curling up and away like smoke, taking whatever meaning they held with them.

The last of the numbers fade and another series of images and sensations moves in to take their place. Asphalt beneath my feet, black and shimmering wet. Lights in the distance. The sound of tires on the road.

My head hums, vibrates like a tuning fork. My ears ring. At least that's what I think at first, but then I realize the sound is coming from outside my head. From outside the trance.

All at once I was back, jolted into the *here* as I remembered where I was. The phone on the counter was ringing. I tried to reach for it, but the phone, the counter, the stores, the mall, *everything* swirled around me, broken up as if torn apart by a cyclone. By the time it all came back together, settling into place piece by piece, the ringing had stopped.

That's when the pain in my hand began to register. I'd been gripping the pencil so tightly my fingers were white from the pressure. The lead dug holes into the paper. My heart sank when I saw the string of numbers written there.

How could it be happening again?

Finally, I was able to let the pencil go and it clattered to the ground. I checked my watch.

8:26.

I'd been out for four minutes. I eyed the area slowly, hoping I hadn't been seen, but I wasn't so lucky.

Standing in the entrance to Kinnear Music was the tie guy.

Staring right at me.

I overheard my mom and dad once, talking about what it was like to see Kyra or me slip into a trance. It didn't sound all that shocking. We'd zone out, stare off into the distance. Sometimes we would tremble just a little. They might not have gotten so upset about it if it wasn't for the writing.

When we're out of it, Kyra and I write numbers. Lots and lots of numbers. Frantically. Intensely. That could be a little harder to watch.

What comes after a trance is worse. Dizziness can last a full minute or two, and it's not easy to hide. Other people started noticing. By middle school, Kyra began explaining the episodes by telling people she and I had a rare genetic form of epilepsy. That seemed to satisfy our teachers and most of our friends.

I realized it didn't really matter what the explanation was, as long as there was one. People just want a way to label what they see. Then they can file it away and forget about it.

So, I figured, as long as I acted normal, the tie guy should forget my four-minute space out. He could chalk it up to me being tired or an idiot or whatever. I forced myself not to look away from him too quickly. Even gave him a little smile. At least I think it was a smile. I couldn't really feel my face.

The mall continued to tilt and sway and I held on to the counter so I wouldn't fall off the stool. That much I think I managed pretty well. Harder to mask was my own shock at what had just happened. I hadn't had a trance since before the accident. In my own naive way, I had hoped the long absence meant the trances wouldn't come anymore.

Worse, even without trying to figure out the meaning of the numbers, I was afraid I knew what the vision was, and it made me shake.

In fact, I couldn't *stop* shaking. I had to get out of the mall before I lost it. There was still half an hour left in my shift before I was supposed to close the kiosk, but that was half an hour too long. I could always tell Carole I got sick. It wasn't far from the truth.

My hands trembled as I stuffed the order forms and receipts into the lockbox under the counter and closed out the register. I didn't know if the tie guy at Kinnear was still watching or not, but I didn't dare look. When I stood, the vertigo hit me again and I stumbled a couple of steps, knocking the stool over. I didn't even try to pick it back up, but grabbed my backpack and dragged the gate around the kiosk, locking it tight.

I'd nearly made it all the way through Nordstrom before the tears began to fall. By the time I got outside, I had to hold my breath to temper the sobs that were clawing their way up my throat. I sat on the edge of one of the oversized planters, covered my face with my hands, and bawled. *Not again*, I thought. *Not again*.

Kyra left home while I was still in the hospital. She went without saying good-bye, without saying anything. Dad said she chose to graduate early. All I knew was that she was gone. I thought maybe that was why the trances had stopped after the accident. Before, the trances had always come to the two of us together. If she wasn't there to complete the circle, I hoped the trances would leave me alone.

I know it's selfish, but that's one reason why I never tried to find out where she was. As much as I loved my sister, as much as I felt a part of me was missing when she was gone, I didn't want the trances back.

Now I had no sister and the trance came anyway. *The wet road, the lights.* Those images were all too real to me; I had seen them the night of the accident. The night my mom died. They were the images I should have seen in the vision Kyra had tried to warn me about. Regret and guilt washed over me again.

I sat on the planter and cried until my head ached. I cried for Kyra, I cried for my mom, and I cried for myself. In a way, all three of us died that night.

"Are you all right?"

The deep voice startled me and I jumped, nearly falling off the planter. It was the tie guy, concern pinching his face. I tried to tell him I was fine, but all that came out of my mouth was an incoherent, "Ugn."

He crouched down in front of me. Up close I could see he had a thin, pale scar just above one cheekbone, and that his green eyes held flecks of gold. "You feeling okay?" he asked again.

I wiped my tears with the back of my hand. "I'm fine," I managed to whisper.

He tilted his head like he thought he might be able to understand better from a different angle. "You need me to call someone for you?"

I sat up straighter and pushed my hair from my eyes, wishing it was darker outside so he couldn't see how swollen and red my face must be. "It's okay," I said. "I'm waiting for the bus."

Just then, Michelle's voice rang out behind me. "There you are! I was just going to see if you needed a r—" She stopped short and stared at the guy crouched in front of me, immediately switching into protector mode. "What's going on?" There was an edge to her voice I recognized. It meant she was a little worried and a lot perturbed. She directed her next demand toward the guy, who was still crouched in front of me. "Who are you?"

He stood and extended his hand, still a salesman apparently. "I'm Jake," he said. "She your friend?"

"Yes." Her voice was guarded. She looked at his hand but didn't shake it. He let it fall to his side.

"You taking her home?" he asked.

She folded her arms tightly. "Excuse me, Jake, but who *are* you?"

"I work here. I was just heading home when I saw her sitting out here alone. She been sick?"

Michelle still looked confused. "I don't think—"

"She didn't look like she was feeling well at the kiosk."

She raised her brows. "You know where she *works*?"

"I work just across from ShutterBugz."

"Oh. Where—"

"Excuse me," I said. "I'm right here." The words came out thick and strangled-sounding.

Michelle and Jake exchanged a glance, allies all of a sudden. They both ignored me.

"Couldn't help but notice she looked a little zoned out earlier."

Michelle nodded. "It's been a tough week."

"I'm leaving." I tried to stand, but black peppered

my vision and I sank back down onto the planter.

Michelle slipped an arm around my shoulders to prop me up and said in a low voice, "I *told* you it was too early to try and come back." She pulled on my arm. "Come on. Let me get you home."

Jake stood awkwardly for a second and then stooped to help her. "Where you parked?"

Michelle gave him one of those looks, sizing him up and, apparently finding him worthy, inclined her head, granting him permission to lend his assistance. "This way." She gestured with her head. "About halfway up the row."

"This is really not necessary," I said, but both of them ignored me.

Michelle led the way to her car and Jake walked close, one arm guiding, but not quite touching me. Neither one of them said a word. At least not out loud. The look on Michelle's face spoke volumes, though. I didn't miss the curious way she watched Jake, or the speculation in her eyes when she looked at me.

When we reached her car, Jake helped Michelle lower me into the front seat. I didn't really need their help to sit, thank you, but at that point it seemed easier to just go along with it than to argue.

After I was situated to her satisfaction, Michelle straightened and held her hand out to Jake. "Thanks for your help."

For half a heartbeat he just looked at her standing there

and I wondered if he would leave her dangling the way she had done to him by the planter, but then he took her hand and shook it briskly. "No problem. Hope she's okay."

Michelle's frown showed how far away from okay she believed me to be. "Thanks," she said. And then almost as an afterthought she added, "It was nice to meet you."

He just smiled and as he did, his eyes met mine like we were sharing an inside joke. Then he walked away.

"Tell me everything," Michelle demanded as we pulled out of the parking lot, eyes alight. "Who was that guy?"

I watched as he disappeared behind the parked cars a couple rows over. "You know as much as I do."

"So what happened? What's wrong? Have you been crying?"

Images of the vision flashed through my head. I closed my eyes, hoping they would disappear. "It's nothing."

She didn't look so sure, but she was willing to let the question drop to move on to more important matters. "So," she said, "Jake's pretty hot."

I let myself smile at that. "I guess so."

"You *guess* so? Are you kidding?" She slid me a sideways look. "So really, you're okay?"

"I'm fine," I said. Just fine.

When we pulled up to the curb in front of my house, all the windows were completely dark. By the way Michelle was frowning, I wondered if she could tell how empty it was inside. Not unoccupied empty. Broken shell empty. And not just when my dad was out of town, either. He'd been traveling more since the accident, but even when he was home, he was gone. You could see it in his eyes whenever he looked at me; he would rather be somewhere else. Anywhere else.

Not that I blamed him.

"Whoa," Michelle said. "Don't look now, but we've got an audience."

Sure enough, across the street stood our neighbor Mrs. Briggs in her usual spot—smack in the middle of her huge picture window—her Wonder Woman pose backlit by the front room television. For as long as I can remember, she's stood in that window, watching our house with the same sour look on her face. I got so used to seeing her there that she'd become a part of the architecture in my mind, like the roofline or the porch columns.

"Should we wave?" Michelle whispered, her hand already rising in parade mode.

I swatted it down. "Don't."

She just laughed and waved with the other hand.

"Seriously."

"Why?" She gave me a sharp look. "What's going on?"

I wasn't sure if I could find all the words it would take to explain it to her—if I had the inclination, which I didn't. I glanced back at my house.

"Wait." Michelle twisted in her seat to face me. "Your dad's gone again, isn't he? He's got her spying on you."

"Don't be dramatic." I felt in the dark for the door handle. "He just asked her to watch out for me while he's away."

"When will he be back?" The pity in her voice was misplaced, as if Dad being gone was the worst thing I had to deal with.

Michelle's dad owns a construction company in town, so he never has to travel for business and she doesn't understand the concept. My dad's a marketing consultant and has clients all over the country, so he's gone a lot. Before my mom died, Michelle hardly ever noticed when he went out of town. Since I got out of the hospital, it was like her missing-parent radar kicked in. I didn't have to talk about him being gone. She just *knew*.

"Tomorrow," I said. "He'll be back in the morning."

She took a moment to digest this. "Do you want me to come in for a little while?"

I forced a laugh. "Would you stop? I'm fine. Really."

"I could stay with you for—"

"Michelle. Give it a rest."

She sat quietly for a moment, trailing a finger along the leather wrap on her steering wheel. "So . . . do you think you'll be up for running in the morning? Because we could take the day off if you need to."

"I don't need a day off. I'll see you at six." I let myself out of the car and hoisted my backpack onto my shoulder.

Michelle leaned across the passenger seat and looked up at me, eyes searching. "If you're sure," she said.

I laughed again and shut the door. "Go, already."

I watched her drive away, my heart dropping a little as her red taillights disappeared around the corner.

Across the street, Mrs. Briggs hadn't moved from her spot in the front room window. As annoying as she was, it was strangely comforting to see her standing there, just like always. Even way back when Kyra and I were little I can remember Mrs. Briggs standing watch. We used to curtsy to her or blow kisses or something to let her know we knew she was watching us. I turned and walked to the house, pausing to unlock the front door. It actually felt good to know that there was one thing in my life that had not changed.

There are rooms in my house I can't go into anymore. I don't mean because those rooms are forbidden. I'm not *physically* able to enter them because they were hers. My legs start to tremble and my palms sweat and my head hums like a chain saw, shooting pain across my skull.

My mom was really into HGTV. She'd watch shows like *Color Splash* and *Myles of Style* and the next thing you knew, she was pulling down curtains to let in the natural light or painting the hallway a vibrant shade of coral.

The front room was one of her pet projects, even though we hardly ever used it. We had a great room at the back of the house where we always hung out, but she wanted a "proper place" to entertain visitors. Not that we had a lot of those—we all kind of kept to ourselves. It's hard to be outgoing when you're ashamed.

Mom called the front room "the parlor," as if we lived in a stately Victorian mansion instead of a tract house in the suburbs. She was always in there—covering a cushion here or adding a flower arrangement there—until she became as much a part of the room as the wingback chair or its matching floral ottoman. Sometimes if I looked just right I could still see her sitting on the couch, thumbing through her *House Beautiful* magazines. She'd hear me in the doorway and glance up, her eyes hollow and sad. All that designing and she couldn't do a thing about her daughters.

Inside, I turned the dead bolt with a *thunk* that echoed through the empty house. As I passed the parlor, I kept my eyes on the speckled pattern of moonlight that danced across the polished wood floor so they wouldn't accidentally stray to the couch—or to the collection of photos on the wall.

One of my mom's many decorating ideas was to create a "living wall" in the front hallway—a collection of family photos in matching frames that showed us in various stages of family life. My favorite picture—and the one I couldn't bring myself to look at anymore—was of Kyra, my mom, and me, taken the summer I turned fifteen. I'd had a sleepover birthday party and my mom had come into my bedroom with us to play cards. She was in one of her good moods that night. She wore a silk kimono my dad had just brought back for her from a business trip to Japan and her usually perfect hair was pulled back with a clip. We were laughing about something—I don't know what, because my dad had taken the picture from the doorway unannounced. I loved the spontaneity of it, though. Mom was sitting between Kyra and me, her legs tucked up beneath her. Our heads bent together like we were sharing a secret. Kyra's hand is half-covering her mouth as if she's trying to hold on to the laughter. The part I liked most about the picture was the contentment in my mom's eyes. Like, if only for that moment, she was just where she wanted to be.

I tiptoed to my room, even though there was no one home to hear me, and paused in the silent doorway. In the moonlight, I could just make out the outline of my desk and of the false-bottom flowerpot that sat on the far corner of it. My dad had bought the flowerpot when he was at a flea market with my mom. He thought we could use it in the kitchen to hide emergency cash or an extra set of keys. Mom said it didn't fit in with the decor and threw the thing away. I felt bad for my dad, so I rescued it from the trash and kept it on my desk to hold loose change. The screw-off bottom section hid other things.

Hesitantly, reluctantly, I crossed to the desk and clicked on the lamp. A small puddle of light washed over the desktop and spilled onto the floor. I pulled out the chair and sat, stalling, stalling until I could make myself reach for the flowerpot. Slowly, I unscrewed the bottom and a handful of folded papers fluttered out. They lay on the desk like little origami nightmares. I drew the latest from my pocket and set it alongside the others and then carefully straightened them all, opening them up to reveal the numbers scrawled across the pages.

The earliest memory I have of the trances is from preschool. I couldn't have been more than four or five years old, standing obediently next to my mom as the teacher showed her paper after paper filled with numbers I had written. The teacher seemed confused. The handwriting didn't look like my tiny hand scrawl. I'd correctly worked long strings of equations though I had a hard time counting in class. It didn't make sense. My mom wouldn't hear it. She kept insisting I had some kind of gift, just like my big sister, Kyra.

It wasn't long after that, though, that our parents took both of us to see our first therapist. Everything in his office was bright and colorful and when he spoke to us, he used a perky voice, like Captain Jack or Barney. But we weren't fooled. We saw the way Mom strangled her handkerchief as she described our writing to the doctor.

We saw how Dad sat stiff in his cheery yellow chair and stared out the window.

The doctor sent my sister and me into a room that had a big mirror-window along one wall. In the middle of the room sat a plastic Fisher-Price table surrounded by little yellow-and-blue chairs. On the table lay an assortment of paper and crayons. The doctor asked us if we wanted to write.

We sat on the chairs but we knew better than to pick up the crayons. In those short moments, we learned to be ashamed of the trances. That's what we heard the doctor call what we did—"trance writing." We didn't know what it meant at first, but we did see how our mother's face crumpled when he said the words. We saw the way she looked at us, her fingers moving over her crucifix. We saw the shame in her eyes. Even though at that time we didn't understand what kind of power our ability held, we knew. Our gift was no longer a gift. It was a curse.

Opening each paper, I flattened them with my hand. On each one, bold equations had been scrawled in a variety of different handwriting. None of them were mine. I ran my finger over the latest numbers, looking for a clue to their meaning even though I knew I would never find one. Kyra and I had been trying to decipher the writing for years. It just didn't make sense.

This note was shorter than a lot of the others had been, just three strings of numbers:

$$1 + 1 + 2 + 5 = 9$$
$$1 + 5 + 4 + 5 + 2 + 3 + 7 + 5 = 32$$
$$3 + 2 = 5$$

The way the numbers appeared looked like the stuff we saw on the numerology sites Kyra had once followed online. She had learned that in numerology, each number represented a letter, so she thought maybe we could use the numerology system to decipher some kind of message in our writing. The problem was, numerology only assigned number values from one through nine, so several letters could share the same number. That worked great if you were assigning numbers to letters in a word you already knew, but not so much if you were trying to work it backward. There were too many possibilities.

As far as we could tell, the numbers didn't seem to fit the configuration for a date or a coordinate, either. We still believed the numbers had to mean something, we just didn't know what it was. Or why they came to us. We both felt like we were supposed to be doing something to prevent the things we saw, but without a clear direction, how were we supposed to do that? Bad things happened and people got hurt and there was nothing we could do.

I folded the notes again and hid them back in the flowerpot, an empty ache gnawing at my chest. I didn't want the trances back again. I couldn't stand the responsibility or the pain. For whatever reason, they had stopped once. I needed them to stop again.

Twisting around in my chair, I looked at Kyra's empty bed against the far wall. Moonlight from the window stretched across the room and rested on it like a spotlight. The bed was made up just the way she left it, except that the quilt she used to keep folded at the foot of the bed was gone and the pillow had long since lost the indent from her head.

My stomach felt hollow, like it did whenever I thought of Kyra being gone, but now another sensation filled the empty space. It felt like desperation. We had always received the trances together. Now I was on my own. It scared me.

Suddenly, I felt like a lost little kid and I longed more than ever for Kyra to come home. I switched off the desk light and, without even bothering to get undressed, curled up on my bed, fighting back the tears. Words from an old nursery rhyme Kyra and I used to sing swirled through my head. I stared at the wall but in my mind I saw Kyra jumping rope out on the playground at our elementary school, singing to the rhythm as the rope swept under her feet.

Two little
Swish!
angels
Swish!
dressed in
Swish!
white
Swish!
try to get to
Swish!
heaven on the
Swish!
end of a kite
My lips moved silently as I finished the song. "The kite string broke and down they fell and instead of heaven, they went to hell."

I squeezed my eyes tight against the fresh tears that were forming. Kyra always liked that song. I never understood why.

5

When I woke up, the band of moonlight had moved on to the wall at the far side of the room. I swung my legs over the edge of the bed and sat for a long time, staring into the shadows.

I kept thinking of those long weeks in the hospital. I never had any trances while I was there. And after I got home, nothing. It's like the accident had flipped a switch and turned them off. I had never wanted to look too closely at *why* they stopped because I was afraid if I did, they might start up again.

In the end it didn't matter; the switch had been thrown anyway. The trances were back. For years, Kyra and I had tried to find a way to stop the trances from coming. Now that I knew it was possible, I was determined to find a way to make them stop again.

There were certain constants about the trances I knew I could rely on. Like what happened when Kyra or I slipped into one. We would see flashes, tiny glimpses of things that were going to happen. Even when Kyra and I would piece together the images we saw, it was never enough to see the whole picture. We never knew what it meant, but we did know whatever was coming would not be good.

The "warnings" always involved someone we knew, or had at least met. Sometimes we saw who it was before the event, sometimes we could only guess. That's what we figured the numbers were for—to fill in the missing information.

The numbers were another constant. We never did slip into a trance without writing them. Often Kyra and I would write the same equations, even though the things we saw were different.

Also, until the night before the accident, the trances had always pulled Kyra and me in at the same time. That's why I figured the trances had quit; because Kyra wasn't with me anymore. I always assumed it took the two of us together for the trances to happen, but last night proved that theory to be wrong.

But then, of course, it had been wrong before. Only one of us had seen the trance I missed the night before my mother was killed.

I pushed up from the bed and padded into the bathroom, not even bothering to turn on the light. In the darkness

I scrubbed my teeth and splashed water on my face. Pressing a cool washcloth over my aching eyes, I tried to push away the image of that dark road, the glistening pavement, the headlights bearing down on me.

Last night's vision was eerily close to the real-life accident that killed my mom. Could it have been the scene I should have seen months ago? No, that didn't make sense. Kyra and I never saw visions of events that already happened. But everything was different now. I didn't know what to expect.

I returned to my bed and lay down, pulling the covers up to my neck. I tried to shut off my brain and go back to sleep, but my attention kept being pulled to Kyra's empty bed. It sat there in the shadows like an accusation, the silence screaming in my head. If only I had listened to her . . .

I couldn't take it. I grabbed my backpack and escaped to the kitchen, settling into one of the chairs at the table. May as well get my homework done since I didn't even look at it when I was at work. A little pang tightened my stomach when I thought of my disastrous first night at the mall. I reached for my trig homework and dug in. If anything could make my mind go numb, math could. I searched for derivatives until my head felt heavy and I couldn't focus on the symbols anymore. I rested my head on my folded arms and before I knew it, I was gone.

***

A sound outside my dream jerked me awake and I sat up, blinking and rubbing my eyes. My textbook was still on the kitchen table, but the study guide had fallen to the floor. I was bending to pick it up when I heard the sound again. Then a shadow moved just outside the sliding glass door. I straightened slowly, staring at the dark shape, barely daring to breathe.

"Lynnie, it's me." Michelle rapped on the glass.

I clutched at my chest where my heart was skittering like a scared rabbit. "What are you *doing* out there?" I demanded.

"I tried the front door but you didn't answer." She tapped the glass again. "Are you going to let me in or what? It's cold!"

Just as I was about to get up and open the door for her, Michelle slid it open and stepped inside.

"Did you know this thing was unlocked?" She closed the door behind her and clicked the little latch. "Not that the lock is going to do you much good . . . My aunt had a sliding door in her apartment and one time this guy came with a crowbar and pried it right out of the—" She cut herself off and gave me an exasperated look. "What?"

I shook my head. "Thanks for making me feel so secure."

She cocked her hip and planted one hand on it. "Hey, if it's true, it's true. Since you're home alone so much, I just thought you should be aware."

"You're very thoughtful."

"I know." She grinned at me until she noticed my open books on the table. "Don't tell me you fell asleep studying."

"Okay. I won't."

"You still up for a run?"

I glanced at the clock. 6:03. "Give me a minute," I said, already turning toward the hallway. "I'll get changed."

In my room, I pulled on my running clothes, trying not to let myself dwell on the fact that Kyra was gone. The familiar dull ache hollowed out my chest whenever I thought about her. Most days I tried to accept that she needed time to herself, but after my solo trance, her absence was too much. I needed to talk to her; she was the only one who could possibly understand. Except she didn't want me to know where she was.

I grabbed my shoes and hurried down the hall to the front door in stocking feet. Michelle had gone out to begin stretching as I put on my shoes. Outside the parlor window, the sky was a wash of deep peaches and purples. The predawn glow cast reverse shadows across my mom's couch. I shut my eyes to the sight of it and stepped outside, closing the door firmly behind me.

Running was really my dad's thing. He was a star sprinter in college and one of the only times I ever heard him get excited about anything was when he talked about the high he got when his muscles were pumping and the wind was blowing back his hair. I was still pretty young when I figured out I could get more time with my dad if I said I loved running, too.

The morning run used to be our special time. We never said much, but just being together and sharing the sunrise was enough. One morning we raced the last couple of blocks and Dad discovered I could be fast when I wanted to be. He started talking college and scholarships and the next thing I knew, I was joining the track team and he was cheering me on.

Until the accident. I hadn't seen him run at all since I got home from the hospital. I asked him plenty of times if he wanted to join me, but he always had something to do. I kept going, hoping he would notice. Hoping he could still be proud of me. Hoping I could make him forget what I had done.

My dad and I had a thing when we ran together—we didn't say a word to each other for at least the first couple blocks because that's usually how long it takes to work the kinks out and fall into your stride. When Michelle started running with me in his place, this was a hard habit for her to get used to. Michelle's a talker. For her, keeping quiet for two feet was a challenge, let alone two blocks. The way she kept glancing over at me that morning, I could tell she wasn't going to make it that far. Sure enough, we barely reached the end of the block before she cleared her throat.

"That was interesting last night."

"Tell me about it."

Our feet hit the asphalt in a steady rhythm. *Thunk. Thunk. Thunk.*

"Aren't you even the least bit intrigued that the music guy was watching you?"

"His name is Jake, and he wasn't watching me."

She rolled her eyes. "Right. He just happened to notice you weren't feeling well. *And* followed you outside."

I didn't want to encourage her by answering, but I couldn't help myself. "He did not follow me outside. He was on his way home."

"Uh-huh."

"And it's not like he had to *watch* anything. The kiosk is right there in the middle of the walkway. Kind of hard to miss."

"Methinks," she said haughtily, "you do protest too much."

"Nice misquote." I shot her a look. "Shakespeare just rolled over in his grave."

Michelle laughed. "And you are avoiding the issue."

"There is no issue," I said testily. "Can we just drop it?"

Thunk. Thunk. Thunk.

"All right, then." She must have realized she wasn't going to get anything out of me, because she shifted gears without missing a beat and kept on talking. "Trey and I ran into some of the guys at the movies last night—"

"Hold on. You and Trey finally went out? When did this happen?"

"We didn't go *out*," she said, avoiding the question. "He met me at the theater."

"Prearranged?" I asked.

She pressed her lips together like she didn't want the word to escape. Finally, she said, "Yes."

I grinned triumphantly. "Date."

"Do you want to know what the guys were saying or what?"

Thunk, thunk, thunk.

"Okay, I give up. What were the guys saying?"

"That Nick Cumberland got pwned last night." She smiled at the thought. Michelle never liked Nick, especially after what she called our "history." "He was trying to come on to some girl and she completely shot him down. Best thing is, she did it right in front of all his friends."

I lost the stride and had to double step a couple of times to find it again. *Come on, Greenfield. We could go someplace quiet.*

"Really."

"Yeah." She smiled like this was her own personal victory. "Eventually nature finds a way to restore the balance."

I bit my lip. That's what I was afraid of.

***

I sat in life sciences, staring out the window at the gray day outside. The memory of my trance the night before had followed me like campfire smoke all morning, clinging to me no matter how much I tried to escape it. It had been short, only a few images, but those images were burned into my brain. The rain, the wet pavement, the headlights of a car. Images I should have seen weeks ago.

"Greenfield. You in there?"

I blinked out of my stupor to find Todd Gibbons snapping his fingers in front of my face.

"What? I'm sorry."

"You got that study sheet you said I could borrow?"

"Oh. Yeah. Hold on." I rifled through my binder and found the paper. "Here it is."

"Thanks." He stuffed it into his textbook, giving me a conspiratorial grin. "Man, what are you *on*?"

I looked up at him sharply. "On?"

"Yeah. You been staring out that window half the class. Didn't even hear the bell ring."

"Oh." I noticed for the first time that everyone else in the class had already gone. "A lot on my mind, I guess."

"If you say so. Might want to be a little smoother about it, if you know what I mean." He hefted his books up under his arm and headed for the door. "Later."

I slapped my notebook shut and stuffed it into my backpack. I hadn't thought anyone would notice if I was a little distracted, but if a burnout like Todd Gibbons called me on it, it must have been obvious. I decided I'd have to be more careful, but as soon as I slung my backpack over my shoulder to go to my next class, the flashes of the night before came flooding back.

The only thing that lifted the gloom a little was remembering that smile from the tie guy, Jake. I should have been mortified that he saw me slip into the trance. I should have been ashamed. But thinking about the way he smiled at me made me feel warm and safe. At least for a moment.

I saw Nick before I even walked through the door for AP lang. He was leaning against a desk right across the aisle from where I usually sat. Like he was waiting for me. My stomach did a little flip, even as it sank. What did he want?

I was already trying to formulate a getaway excuse when he gave me one of those macho chin-jerk acknowledgments and then his eyes moved beyond me. He pushed away from the desk, waving to someone behind me. I turned to see Alicia Hayes coming through the door. She shot me a better-luck-next-time smile and sashayed to the back of the room where Nick and his crowd usually sat. I hugged my books to my chest and sank down on my seat, relieved and, I had to admit, a little bit disappointed.

After all those years, you'd think I would have built up a resistance to the cycle of Nick, but I was still stuck in the never-ending loop of hope and disappointment. Nick had been my first crush, my only make-out, and party to the biggest mistake I had made in my life. And I still liked him.

After school, I changed in the locker room, nervously zipping up my track jacket and tying my shoes. It was the second week of conditioning training for the team, but only my first full day back to practice. My dad was actually looking forward to it more than I was. It was practically the only thing he ever talked to me about. When he was home, that is.

My dad was all about motivation and goals. Ever since he saw how I could run, he had my track career all laid out in his head. He formulated what kind of stats I'd need for college scholarships, how many races I'd have to win to earn those stats, and how hard I'd have to train to win those races. All those weeks I was working on rehab, his main concern seemed to be how soon I could get back out on the track and keep pushing for those goals.

I knew as I worked out that I was chasing his dream, not mine. But I also knew it was the only conversation I could still have with my dad. Don't get me wrong—I love to run, but I want to run for the joy of it, not to beat someone else's time. Still, if it kept Dad happy, I was willing to try.

After the team warmed up, Coach Mendenhall called me over. "We need to time the one-hundred and three-hundred-meter hurdles," he said. "I'd like you to assist Coach Roberts in recording times."

I opened my mouth to protest, but he cut me off. "Look, Greenfield, I appreciate your dedication. I know you've been working hard to get back into shape. But I've been watching you warm up. You're still favoring your right leg."

"No. It's just—"

"You'll assist Coach Roberts this afternoon and we'll talk tomorrow."

What else could I do? I followed the assistant coach to the other side of the field. Michelle was on the track warming up for hurdles and gave me the "what's up?" gesture. I shrugged and made a helpless face.

Coach Roberts pressed the clipboard into my hands and turned to signal the first runner—Justin Allred—to take his mark, get set . . . She blew her whistle and Justin took off. He flew down the track, taking the hurdles and the steps between in perfect rhythm. She announced his time and I wrote it down as she signaled the next runner.

We'd only recorded three times before it hit. All of a sudden came a *whoosh* like a great rush of wind and then I was falling into a vortex.

Not here. Not now.

I tried desperately to breathe through it, even though I knew that wouldn't work. The coach's face swam before my eyes. Distant. Out of focus.

"Greenfield—" she began.

But I was already gone.

The backdrop of the stadium flips and the bleachers disappear. The track morphs into a rain-slicked road. In the air around me, a random jumble of numbers drift and swirl like tendrils of fog. Twin headlights cut through the darkness, racing toward me. I try to scream, but I can't make a sound.

"Ashlyn!"

In one blink, the stadium swirled back into place. I swayed a little and had to take a step to keep my balance.

"Are you okay?" Coach Roberts was staring at me like I had a third eye. "You look kind of pale."

I started to give her the automatic "I'm fine," but I wasn't. Not by a long shot. "I . . . I'm just . . ." I glanced down at the score sheet in my hand and my knees felt weak. Bold, black numbers sprawled across the paper. Ice settled in the pit of my stomach. How could it be happening again? The trances had never come so close together before. "I think I need to sit down."

I pulled off the top score sheet and handed her the clipboard, walking away before she could ask questions. I couldn't walk in a straight line. It felt like when I was a kid and we used to spin around and around and around until we were dizzy and then try to walk. When I finally reached the stadium steps, I sank down onto the cool metal and rested my head on my knees until the dizziness passed. I couldn't stop the trembling, though.

It didn't make sense. Not only had I been pulled into another trance, but the images were a repeat of what I had seen the day before. A repeat of an accident scene I knew too well.

The wet road. Bright lights stabbing my eyes.

It couldn't be. Kyra and I had never seen the same vision twice. It was like I was seeing my own accident. . . .

I didn't want to follow that thought. If I was just now seeing the images I should have seen before the accident, what did it mean? Would all the trances I had missed for the past several weeks come back to haunt me?

Or just the one that killed my mom?

"Hey, what's going on?" Michelle sat next to me, rubbing my back.

I didn't even realize I was crying until I lifted my head

and felt the wetness on my cheeks. I also didn't realize what a sideshow I had become. The guys on the field stood gawking at us. A group of girls jogging around the track slowed down as they passed by, trying not to be too obvious as they stared. I stared right back until they looked away.

"Do you need me to take you home?" Michelle asked. "I could ask Coach if—"

"No." I sat up straighter and wiped my eyes on the sleeve of my jacket. "It's okay. I'm just having a crappy day."

"Maybe you're trying to do too much too soon," she said. "It's okay if you're not ready to—"

"Really. I'm fine." I pushed off the steps, and then had to grab the railing to steady myself.

"Okay, that's it. I am taking you home. Let's go."

I could have argued, but it wouldn't have done any good now that Michelle had officially moved into the protective big-sister mode. Michelle's only a couple of weeks older than I am, but she's a nurturer by nature. Since she's the youngest in her family of boys, she was more than happy to take over the big-sister role when Kyra left.

If only she knew *why* Kyra left, she might not have been so eager to take her place.

"Looks like your dad's back," Michelle said as she pulled in front of my house. His black Accord was parked in the driveway.

I actually was glad to have him home, even though it probably meant I was going to have to explain why I was home from track early. I started to open the car door and she stopped me.

"Lynnie?" She turned down the radio. "Seriously. If there's anything I can do . . ."

"Thanks," I said, "I'm good." I climbed out of the car, closing the door behind me.

Michelle honked and waved to Mrs. Briggs, who was watching from her window, and drove off.

As I expected, Dad was in his office. I peeked in on the way to my room and found him sitting at his desk, laptop open in front of him, his phone's Bluetooth receiver hooked over his ear. He nodded at me and then gestured toward the Bluetooth so I'd be sure to notice he was busy.

I gave him a smile to let him know I understood and closed his door quietly, tiptoeing down the hall to my room like an obedient daughter. On my bed, I sat and listened to the silence of Dad being home and my chest felt hollow again.

It hadn't always been this way. Dad had never been one to sit down and talk, but we used to do things besides running together. Things that didn't need words. Before the accident, Dad and I would watch movies or go on quiet walks. He used to sit at the table to read the paper while I did my homework. We'd go fishing, build a snowman, whatever. It didn't matter if we said anything; it just mattered that we were together.

Since my mom died, all of that changed. We still never talked, but now the silence was so loud it hurt. Now the words we didn't say built entire fortresses between us.

Among the other lies I told myself while I was working through physical therapy was the one about how if I just kept moving forward, eventually everything would return to normal. I didn't stop to think about how *my* "normal" had never been so great in the first place. I just kept believing, despite all the evidence to the contrary.

On my way to work that Saturday, I called on my power of positive thinking and decided it was going to be a good day. It didn't matter what had happened before; I'd just keep moving forward.

My schedule sheet said I would be working with a girl named Gina. As the bus rumbled and swayed over the speed bumps in the mall parking lot, I resolved that Gina and I would get along perfectly.

That was before I realized who Gina was.

When I got to the kiosk, she was already there opening up. At first I saw her only from behind and nothing about her bracelets or her long dark hair registered. Then she walked out from behind the counter and I groaned. Perfect. The pregnant one with the attitude I'd met on Thursday.

She barely looked at me as she pulled back the chain wall. "Late again," she said.

It took all the willpower I could summon not to roll my eyes. Six hours of this was going to be excruciating. "Your watch must be fast." I held out my wrist to show her mine. "I'm on time."

"Not for the third Saturday before Easter you're not." She waddled back around the front of the kiosk and pulled an apron out from underneath the counter. "We've already got moms waiting."

Sure enough, the play area in the center court was filled with kids in their Sunday best. A couple of the mothers looked back at me with anxious faces, waiting for the signal, I supposed, so they could jockey for the first spot in line.

At the counter, Gina struggled to tie the apron behind her back. The posture made her stomach stick out like she was carrying a watermelon under her shirt. A really big watermelon. For a moment I wondered if I should offer to tie the apron for her, but there was nothing in the set of her face that told me she wanted my help. She managed on her own and started punching the merchant code into the cash register, pausing only long enough to give me a sharp look.

"Well, come on," she said.

I slipped behind the counter and grabbed an apron of my own. The donning of the apron seemed to be some kind of magic signal that we were officially open, because as soon as I slipped the top loop over my head, moms began lining up.

"Get them signed in," Gina said, handing me the clipboard. "I'll set up the equipment."

Without waiting for an answer, she slipped into the back. Right, I thought. Like she had anything to set up. The camera and the umbrellas were stationary.

It didn't matter. I pasted on my good employee smile and set the clipboard on the counter, offering a cup of pens to the first lady in line. "Good morning."

"I sure hope so," she said, filling in her name and number.

"So do I," I mumbled.

"Hmmm?" She glanced up.

"I'm sure it will be."

I hated to admit it, but Gina and I made a good team. We cranked through about fifteen sittings before lunch, which is more than I'd ever done at Polaris—and that included two bathroom breaks for her. I didn't even mind that it was Gina who was doing all the picture-taking. We had a rhythm going for a good three hours with her manning the cameras and me selling the portrait packages.

Finally, we reached the last name on the page and she called out from behind the partition, "Quick! Put up the sign!"

The only sign I knew about was the "BACK IN . . ." sign with the adjustable clock on it. It was something we stuck on the counter when we were working alone to let customers know when we'd be back if we had to run to the bathroom or something. But there were two of us; we could tag team for breaks. I peeked around the fake wall. "Which sign are you talking about?"

She was folding a square of sheer, peach-colored fabric and didn't even look up at me. "What do you mean which sign? The Be Back sign. How many signs are there?"

I hesitated. "Well, it's just—"

"Don't you want lunch?" She tucked the fabric into a three-tiered plastic box that looked like the kind of thing my mom used to organize her craft supplies.

"Well, yeah, but since there's two of us . . ."

She snapped the box closed and picked it up by its sparkly purple handle. "Excuse me," she said, gesturing for me to move out of the "doorway." She slid her box under the counter and grabbed the countertop sign, adjusting the little plastic minute hands to show half an hour. Then she turned to face me. "On a busy day like today, it takes two of us to keep things moving."

"But it's slowed down now. I could take over when—"

Gina shook her head. "I'm sure *you* could. But I sure as hell don't want to take a shift alone while you go on your break, so we're going to close up shop." She reached under the counter once more and came back up with her leather bag. "Are you coming or what?"

Her invitation surprised me. If it *was* an invitation. Usually, I took my lunch alone, but I thought of my resolve before coming to work, and followed her to the food court.

We didn't make it three steps inside before Gina stopped to dig through her bag. "I gotta hit the john." She handed me a twenty. "Grab me some bourbon chicken, would you? Not the whole meal, just the chicken. And a large lemonade. No, make that a medium or else I'll be going all afternoon."

Naturally, Boutin's Cajun Grill had the longest line in the whole food court. I grumbled to myself and joined the crowd, which already wound halfway back to the Rolling Scone. And here I thought Gina had invited me to join her for the company. From my spot in line, I watched her wobble past tables and chairs on her way to the ladies' room. She could have at least said "please."

By the time I made it through the line, Gina had returned from the restroom and had found an empty table. She settled in, feet propped on one of the empty chairs. I set the tray onto the table and sank down on the chair across from her.

"Oh, yesss." She grabbed her lemonade and took a huge swig. "I've had cotton mouth all morning."

I pointed out her change on the tray and she tucked it into her purse before spreading a napkin over the top of her stomach. "So . . ." She speared a piece of chicken with her fork. "Tell me, Ashlyn. What's your story?"

I'd been peeling back the paper wrapper on my straw and I froze, mid-peel. "What do you mean?"

"Whoa. That was quite a reaction. What I *meant*," she said, emphasizing the word, "was how did Carole rope you into working for her? But I'm guessing you have more interesting stories to tell." She took another sip of her lemonade, her eyes never leaving me.

I finished unwrapping my straw and stirred the ice around in my water with it. "Sorry to disappoint you. Nothing exciting here. How about you? When is your baby due?"

Both her hands smoothed over her belly and a small smile touched her lips. "Five more weeks. Nice diversion, by the way."

"Then you'll like this even better. Boy or girl?"

She laughed. "Excellent technique. And I'm not telling."

"But you know?"

Another belly rub. "Yeah. I'm not one of those who think you have to wait until the baby pops out to see what it is so you can be surprised. I mean, what's the purpose of that? So I did all the usual stuff early on, dousing, tarot, bibliomancy, and . . . don't raise your eyebrows at me like that!" She swatted me with her napkin.

"I wasn't!" I said. In fact, the picture of Gina dangling

something over her stomach to guess the sex of the baby was more fascinating than surprising.

"I happen to have faith in the divine," she continued, "which is more than I can say for the daddy."

"He didn't believe your readings?"

She took a sip of her lemonade, shaking her head. "Nah. But once I told him what I found out, he wanted scientific proof, so we had to spring for the ultrasound."

"But it's a secret."

"Yeah. He still likes the surprise angle, so we decided to compromise and keep everyone else in the dark."

"But then you'll get all unisex stuff at your shower," I reasoned.

Her smile faded and she looked away. "Nah. I don't have to worry about that."

Before I could ask her what she meant, I noticed Jake the music store guy weaving through the crowded maze of tables. He was wearing the same awful music-note tie, but paired with a denim shirt this time. And he was headed our way. I dropped my eyes to my cup and slid down in my chair. I had hoped never to face him again after what happened on Thursday. He must have thought I was the biggest freak.

When I peeked up again he was looking straight at me and flashed me a smile. A very nice smile. Gina must have noticed me looking behind her because she twisted in her seat to see what it was—as much as her shape would allow, anyway.

Her face lit up when she saw Jake and she waved him over. "Hey, lover!"

He lifted his chin in response. "How's it going, gorgeous?"

"Come take a load off." She patted the remaining empty chair at our table.

"There's an offer I can't refuse." He turned his smile back to me as he took his seat, setting a brown paper sack and a water bottle on the table. "Feeling better?"

"And here I was about to introduce you." Gina looked from Jake to me. "You two know each other? Do tell."

I waited for him to say something since he and Gina were obviously friends, but he just looked at me with the same expectant expression Gina was wearing.

"We met the other night," I said finally. "He . . . came to my rescue, not once but twice."

"Oh?" She turned her attention back to him. "Rescuing damsels in distress? How very gallant."

He spread his hands. "What can I tell you? I'm a catch."

"That's what you keep saying." Gina nudged his arm with a kind of comfortable familiarity I envied. "So where's your lunch?"

He held up his paper sack. "Some of us are on a budget."

"Maybe *some of us* don't need new two-thousand-dollar amps. You need to eat!" She reached over and pinched his arm. "Look at this! Skin and bones. I'm telling you, you want to maintain your manly physique, you've got to indulge in mall food once in a while."

I personally didn't think there was anything wrong with his physique, but I kept those thoughts to myself. It wasn't my conversation. I stirred my salad around with my fork, listening to them joke back and forth.

"Well, kids, that's it," Gina said finally, pushing back from the table as she struggled to her feet. "We're back on in ten and I gotta pee something fierce." She grabbed her lemonade and used it as a pointer that she leveled at Jake. "Take care of my girl. Don't keep her out late."

He saluted. "Yes, ma'am."

She lumbered back toward the restroom leaving Jake and me alone at the table. Suddenly, I didn't know what to do with myself. I picked up my water then put it back again, checked my watch out of habit.

"Don't worry. You have time."

I glanced up at him. "Huh?"

He gestured to my salad. "To finish your lunch. Didn't Gina say you had ten minutes?"

"Oh. Yeah." I picked up my fork. "You sure bring out a different side of her."

He laughed. "What, Gina? Gina doesn't have sides. She's just . . . Gina."

I considered that for a moment. "What does that mean, 'just Gina'?"

He shrugged and opened up his paper bag, pulling out a

sandwich in a Ziploc baggie. "I don't know. Crazy. Genuine. Real. With Gina, what you see is what you get."

"Oh." I wondered how people would describe me. Crazy, maybe, but genuine? I don't think so. Real? I'd gotten so used to lying to cover my secret over the years that I wasn't even sure I knew what real was. I toyed with my lettuce some more.

"Yeah. You just have to stay out of her way sometimes." Jake took a bite of his sandwich and grimaced. "Man, I really should learn to cook."

I eyed the soggy mess in his hand. "What've you got there?"

He lifted the top piece of bread to reveal the pinkish-brown paste underneath. "Tuna. It's all we had."

"Looks like maybe you didn't drain it very well."

"Drain it?" He examined the sandwich and frowned.

"Here." I slid my tray over in front of him. "You can have my salad. I'm not really hungry."

Jake put down his sandwich slowly. "You're . . . giving me your salad?"

"If you want it," I said in a small voice. "Blackened shrimp. Cajun. It's good." I forced a smile, but inside I was kicking myself. What was I thinking? Offering to share food was way too familiar. He probably thought I was coming on to him or something. The heat rose in my face again, only quicker this time.

He just grinned. "I've never gotten a salad from a girl

before." He practically purred, drawling the word so that it sounded like *guurrrl*.

"Well." I took a sip of my water to hide the immense relief from showing on my face. "Just don't let it go to your head."

"Never," he said solemnly.

The conversation lagged and I guessed it was my turn to say something. But really? I wasn't any good at the back-and-forth. I hadn't had much practice. "Um . . . so you're really good," I blurted.

He was taking a bite of the salad and paused with the fork halfway to his mouth. "Only on Sundays," he dead-panned.

"On the piano," I clarified, my face practically combustible.

He chewed for a moment. Swallowed and smiled. "Thanks. Gotta sell those Wurlitzers." I must have really looked lost because he added, "It's my uncle's store. He swears he makes more sales if customers can see the pianos in use."

"I see. Just in case they haven't figured out what to do with one before stumbling into his store?"

"Exactly. And what about you? Tell me something about yourself."

I actually thought for a moment. As if I could come up with anything worth telling. The truth was, I couldn't tell him anything. I had no business sitting there, flirting with

him. Why start something that could never go anywhere?
"You know what?" I said. "I've got to get back to work."

His smile faded and was replaced with confusion.

"I'm sorry. I . . ." I pushed away from the table and
jumped to my feet. "I should go."

The confusion turned into a frown. "See you later,
then."

"Right. Later."

I hurried from the food court, feeling his eyes on me the
entire way.

G ina was just getting back to the kiosk at the same time I was. "Naptime's over," she said, gesturing with her head toward the hordes of toddlers in bow ties and pink frills playing on the pressed-foam ice cream in the center court. She stuffed the Be Back sign under the counter and grabbed her craft box, pausing long enough to throw me an impatient look over her shoulder. "Well, come on. We don't have much time."

I followed her to the back section of the kiosk, wondering what happened to the cheerful, joking Gina I had seen at lunch. Jake said she didn't have sides, but I wasn't so sure. "What are we doing?"

She opened the box and began pulling things out, piling them on the table. "I'm going to show you the arsenal," she said without glancing up. "I've got to get off my feet. Look at this." She lifted one foot in illustration. "My ankles are as big as my thighs. I'm going to take over the front counter for a while and you can do the portraits."

"Sure," I answered, although I knew she wasn't really asking for my consent.

Gina pulled the length of sheer, peachy fabric from the box. "This is for filtering the light," she said. "Let it drape over the umbrellas. Yes. Like that. Kind of like a makeshift light box. And this"—she held up a dime-store up-light— "put it under the table to provide a little backlighting so the kids won't end up looking like paper cutouts against the backdrop."

I took the light and turned it over in my hands. "How did you come up with—"

She just *hmmphed* and pulled out a homemade lens filter from her box. "If I have to work with this artless medium, at least I can try to give it some authenticity. I mean, do you like taking these kind of pictures?"

"You mean posed, flat, and fake?"

"Exactly."

I shrugged. My kind of photography wasn't the studio variety. I didn't know much about taking portraits, besides what I had learned from Carole—but I did know they had no life to them. They didn't look real. But then, there weren't a whole lot of options to change things with the setup Carole had. I said so to Gina and she *hmmphed* again.

"Never use limitations as an excuse for mediocrity," she said, and left me to set up the lights.

Music floated over the confusion of Saturday afternoon shoppers and I looked up to see Jake back at the piano in Kinnear's window. His eyes were closed and he rocked gently to the tempo of the song he was playing. I recognized the music. Something classical, but I couldn't remember the composer. The way he played it, though, was entirely new to me—heartbreaking and hopeful at the same time.

I stopped what I was doing and watched him until the song was over. After the final note, he sat still, fingers resting on the keys. It was almost as if he had to gather himself after the music the way I did after a trance. Then he lifted his head and his eyes met mine. A slow smile touched his lips and he dipped his head.

Heat rose in my cheeks and I quickly turned back to the lights. *Don't,* I warned myself. *Don't even start.*

We had a steady flow of kids until about three-thirty, when it began to taper off. Only two screamers and half a dozen criers in total. When we hit a lull, I wandered up front to find Gina still perched on the stool, one hand pressing on the small of her back as she studied something that was lying on the counter.

"Gina?"

Whatever it was on the counter, she hurried and stuffed it into her pocket and swiped at her eyes with the back of her hand before turning to face me. "Damn hormones." Her laugh sounded like it got caught in her throat. "I'm turning into some kind of schizoid with all these mood swings."

I felt like I had walked in on a private moment and I didn't know how to get myself back out again. I wondered if I should offer some kind of comfort, but then I wasn't sure if she might think of it as an intrusion. I remembered how I'd hated the empty platitudes of friends who thought they should "say something" after my mom died. Maybe it would be better not to mention the tears. "Uh . . . how much time until the next sign-in?"

"Enough time for me to hit the john," she said, her voice all attitude again. She eased herself off the stool. "I swear, my bladder's squashed flat as a pancake."

She pushed past me and rushed off toward the food-court bathrooms, one hand cupping her mouth. Jake was wrong if he thought Gina was an open book. Everyone has secrets they hold inside. Some people are just better at it than others.

After work I was supposed to meet Michelle by the Nordstrom entrance so we could go to Wal-Mart and look at running bras together. That was not something I was going to do with my dad. She wasn't waiting when I got there, but that didn't worry me much; Michelle had never been uptight about being on time. She'd just shrug and say that time was relative.

Fifteen minutes later, though, I was starting to wonder where she was. Relative is one thing, but eventually late is late. Besides, it was getting cold outside now that the sun had gone down. At least my shivering gave me something to worry about instead of the trances. Since we had been so busy at the kiosk, I had made it through the afternoon without fixating on it too much, but all this standing around and waiting was like an open invitation to obsess.

I clamped my hands under my armpits and paced up and down the sidewalk in front of the entrance, worrying. Maybe I should skip Wal-Mart and get home before it happened again. Maybe I should call Michelle. I must have looked like a crazy person, stomping back and forth, muttering. At least, that was my thought when I noticed Jake at the door, watching me as he pushed his way outside.

"Ashlyn?"

I stopped pacing and let my hands drop to my side. "Hi."

He took a step toward me, tentatively, warily, as if I was a patient in an asylum and he was afraid I might snap if he got too close. "Everything all right?"

"Sure," I said. "I'm just wait—"

My cell phone rang.

"I can let that go," I said at the same time as he said, "Go ahead, take it."

I hesitated and he repeated, "Go ahead."

I grabbed the phone from my pocket. Michelle's picture flashed on my screen. I pressed the phone to my ear. "Hello?"

"Oh, Lynnie, I'm so sorry!" she gushed. "I just now realized what time it was. Trey came over and I lost track of—"

"Wait. *Trey* is with you?"

She was silent for a moment and then finally admitted, "Yes."

"Ha! I knew it. You guys are an item."

"We are *not!*" She was half-whispering now and I could imagine her cupping her hand over the phone and turning her back so Trey couldn't hear the conversation. "He came over to study and now we're just hanging out."

"Sure you are."

"Look, do want me to come meet you or not? I can be there in ten."

I laughed. "Are you kidding? Don't you dare leave him. I'll take the bus home."

"But I feel so *bad*," she said, even though I could hear the relief in her voice. "Are you sure? How are you doing? If you're not feeling well . . ."

It was my turn to lower my voice. "I told you. I'm fine. Don't worry about me." She demurred a little bit more, but I assured her it was no problem and she finally hung up.

"Your ride?" Jake asked.

I shrugged and gave him a wouldn't-you-know-it smile as I tucked my phone away. "Hot study date."

"Where do you live? I can take you."

I took a step back. "Oh, no. That's okay. My house is right on the bus line, so . . ."

"I don't mind."

I hesitated. It was just a ride, so why did the thought of it put me so on edge? It's not that I didn't trust Jake or anything. I know I had barely met him, but in a weird way, I felt like I knew him better than half the guys at my school. Watching him play the piano was like peeking into his soul. There was anger—I saw that the first night before Uptight Guy made him play a different song—but there was also beauty. And honesty. That was the constant. Even when he was playing the elevator music, you knew exactly how he felt about it. I gave in. "Thanks. If it's no problem, that would be great."

"No problem at all." He started off across the parking lot and I hurried to keep up with him. "As long as you don't mind helmet hair."

"Helmet?"

He stopped next to a beat-up motorcycle and jangled his keys. "I'm a safety-first kind of guy."

It took a moment to register. I recognized this motorcycle. I'd seen it before, when Michelle was bringing me to Westfield that first night. My mouth dropped open.

The work-of-art motorcycle. Which meant that Jake was the guy Michelle and I had been panting over.

Sure enough, he pulled the bowl helmet from the cargo space and handed it to me. I couldn't even look at him as I took it, remembering him riding alongside the car—how I had admired the lines of his body, the way his muscles had moved, the perfect rear view we'd had when he pulled in front of us. My face must have been Day-Glo pink, it was burning so hot.

Fortunately, Jake didn't seem to notice. He pulled out another helmet—this one black with a scratched-up skull emblem on the back. He smashed it down over his hair and fastened the strap.

"So this is your motorcycle," I said stupidly.

"Not just a 'motorcycle,'" he corrected. "An Indian Trailblazer. Vintage."

"I see. Vintage. Isn't that just a polite way of saying old?"

He ran his hand over the gas tank, where the word *Indian* was painted in script letters on the side. "You say that now, but just wait until she's restored."

I stuck the helmet on my head and Jake laughed.

"You've got it backward," he said. "Here." Before I could react, he reached up and turned the helmet around. Then adjusted the chin strap and fastened it. His fingers brushed my cheek and I was sure he must have felt the heat of my blush.

I tried to swallow, but my mouth was completely dry. "Thanks."

"Anytime." He straddled the bike and patted the space behind him. "Climb on."

I took a deep breath and swung my leg over the bike, settling awkwardly onto the seat. Every point of contact between my legs and his burned like fanned embers. I was grateful he was in front of me so he couldn't see the blush I could feel spreading across my face.

It took him three kicks before the engine roared to life. He gripped the throttle, revved it a couple of times, and yelled, "Hold on!"

I could barely hear him, but I tentatively snaked one arm around his waist, hoping that was what he had suggested. He said something else that sounded like "no backrests" and grabbed my other hand, bringing it around his middle, where he laid it atop the first.

At first, I sat straight-backed and stiff, barely daring to move. I'd never held on to a guy like that before. His muscles beneath my hands felt unyielding and unfamiliar, but at the same time solid and comforting. I had to make myself relax and lean into him to keep my balance. When I did, the thrill I felt in the pit of my stomach was strange and exciting.

I shouted directions to Jake as we rumbled down the streets, but he couldn't hear me over the wind and the engine. Our conversation sounded something like, "Turn left here!" "What?" "Go straight at the light!" "What?" "I really could have taken the bus." "What?"

Finally, we both gave up and I just pointed as we neared each intersection so he would know which way to go.

I got so I could anticipate the tilt of the motorcycle whenever we turned. After a while, I didn't even have to think about it, but just moved with the bike. I closed my eyes, wanting nothing more than to let the wind wash over my face, my skin, my hair.

In that moment, I almost believed I belonged to the world where such simple joys were accepted without question. I felt like I could let down my guard and be myself. I felt free.

But the moment ended as soon as I remembered the last time I let my guard down. That was with Nick. It hadn't turned out so well.

Suddenly, I felt very conspicuous, like anyone looking on would know I didn't belong with a normal guy like Jake. All it would take was another trance in front of him and he would know it, too.

By the time we reached my street, I just wanted to slink off and hide. I pointed out my house and he pulled over to the curb, engine idling as he rested one foot on the ground. Across the street, Mrs. Briggs took up her position in front of her window. I scrambled off the bike.

"Thanks for the ride!" I said.

He just sat there looking at me. I stepped back and

consciously made my mouth curve up into a smile. Still, he didn't leave.

"I appreciate it," I added.

He nodded, but he kept watching me.

"What?" I demanded.

"The helmet." He gestured to my head.

"Oh." I unfastened the chin strap and I handed it to him. His fingers brushed mine as he took it from me, and I jerked my hand away.

He gave me a strange look and drew in a breath like he was about to say something.

I beat him to it. "Thanks again," I said, then I spun around and ran.

8

That night I sat at my desk with my homework spread in front of me, but I couldn't concentrate on anything. I kept replaying my ride home with Jake, reliving the part where I ran away. He must have thought I was such an idiot.

If only I could be sure I had everything under control. If I knew I wouldn't suddenly get sucked into a trance in front of him, I wouldn't be so nervous.

I still didn't understand how the trance at track practice could have come so quickly after the one that happened at work, or why the vision I saw seemed to be an exact rerun of the one I'd seen the day before, but something was definitely different about those trances. I was afraid I knew what it was.

I glanced over at Kyra's side of the room. It made sense

in a twisted sort of way. It had always taken both of us to piece the pictures together, but I hadn't done my part the night before my mom died, so the picture was never completed. The visions I was being shown were the images I should have seen with her.

Maybe there was something I was still missing, something that would complete the picture. But to figure it out, I needed Kyra, and I didn't know where she was. The trance could keep coming back to me again and again and again. The thought made my stomach twist. I had to find Kyra if I had any chance of making it stop.

The problem was, I had no idea where to begin. Dad never spoke about Kyra leaving. The one time he even mentioned it, he said only that she didn't leave a forwarding address. She just moved out. No good-byes, no anything. She didn't even take her cell phone so that I could call and talk to her. She could be anywhere. Where was I supposed to look?

I crossed to her dresser and pulled out the drawers one by one. She hadn't left much behind—I already knew that, but I hoped there would be *something* that would spark an idea. I didn't find a thing. Same with the boxes under her bed. All that was left were a couple of old yearbooks and some folded sweaters.

I searched the bathroom. The desk. The bookshelves. Finally, the only place left to look was our closet. I crossed to the door slowly, pulled it open. *Please,* I thought. *Please, please, please . . .*

***

Another school year has begun. Kyra's in seventh grade, I'm in sixth. I'm sitting at the desk doing my homework when I hear a noise in our closet. I open the door to find Kyra huddled in the corner, knees pulled up tight against her chest. Something is wrong but she won't talk about it.

"Please," I beg. "Tell me what happened."

She only stares into the shadows. Her face is pale and her eyes swollen and red from crying.

"What happened?" I ask again.

"I told," she whispers.

I crawl into the tiny space beside her and close the door behind me. "You what?"

"I told Janelle."

Two days before, we had seen her friend Janelle's dad in a vision. We didn't see what was coming, but we knew something was going to happen to him. Something bad. Kyra desperately tried to make sense of the numbers we'd written so we could warn him. Did they represent a date? A location? We didn't fig-ure it out in time.

"We said we'd never tell anyone," I hiss. "We said we'd keep the trances a secret."

"She was my best friend. I had to tell her what I saw."

My heart drops when I realize she just spoke of

her friend in past tense. I can't see her in the dark of the closet, but I find her hand and hold it. "What happened?" I whisper.

"She laughed." Kyra sniffles softly. "She didn't believe me. So I tried to tell her again and she got mad."

"She's just stupid," I say. I'm trying to make Kyra feel better, but it only makes her cry harder.

"She didn't understand."

"Yeah? Well, how will she like it when—"

"Ashlyn," Kyra says softly, "Janelle's dad had a heart attack. He's dead."

My mouth goes dry and I feel a cold chill snake down my back. "What? When?"

"L-l-last night." Kyra is full on sobbing now. "They found him this morning."

The air in the closet feels stale and thin. "We didn't know," I say, as much to myself as to her. "There's nothing we—"

"Sh-she said I was a witch," Kyra cries.

"Who?"

"Janelle's mom. Janelle told h-her what I said and her mom s-s-said I was the spawn of Satan. She called Mom and said I'm not allowed in their house anymore."

Burning shame and anger fight inside me, but I try to laugh it off. "She actually said that? 'Spawn of

Satan'? What does that make me, Sister of Spawn?"
My sad attempt at humor is lost on Kyra.
"It hurts," she says.
"I know," I say softly. "I know."

That summer was the last time I remember Kyra ever having a close friend. She started pulling away after that, folding in on herself smaller and smaller until she could have disappeared altogether. She kept to herself at school, never went out, even when I tried to get her to do things with me.

Sometimes I would see her watching other people—friends laughing, couples holding hands—and her eyes would go dead. To her, relationships were something to be avoided. To me, they were something to achieve. She wanted to be left alone. I wanted to belong.

We couldn't have known it then, but that moment in the closet set about a series of changes in us both that ended with her hiding away in some apartment somewhere and me, desperate to find her, rummaging through her things.

On the closet shelf were three plastic boxes of Kyra's stuff and I yanked them out onto the floor one by one so I could go through them. As far as I could tell, they were nothing but junk—an old iPod, some books Kyra had to read for Honors English, a couple of notebooks, old school papers. That's probably why she left it behind.

I flipped through all the pages just to be sure, desperate for a mention, a clue, anything that would tell me where she had gone. There was nothing.

When I tried to push the last box back up onto the shelf, it wouldn't slide into place. Something was in the way. I dropped the box and stood on my tiptoes to feel for whatever it was, excited and hopeful that I had finally found something of use.

What I found instead was my old journal, covered in a fine layer of dust. My breath caught when I turned it over in my hands. I hadn't even thought about it since before the accident. I hadn't wanted to.

My journal was a record of happy times and there hadn't been many of those since my mom died. I wiped the dust off with my sleeve and carried the book to my bed. For a long time, I just sat and looked at the cover. In a way, I was afraid to look through the pages, afraid that the memories would be too painful.

Just then, I heard my dad's office door open. Finally! I jumped off the bed and hurried to ask him about Kyra.

When I reached the kitchen, he was standing by the open fridge, pouring himself a glass of juice.

"Dad?" I said. "Where did—"

But he held a finger to his lips and then pointed to the Bluetooth, still attached to his head. He closed the fridge and walked back to the office, shutting his door behind him.

I stared after him. Fine. If I had to camp outside his office door I would. Sooner or later he would have to get off of the phone and when he did, I'd be there.

I dropped onto the couch facing his door to watch and wait. And wait. The journal fell open on my lap and I allowed myself to thumb through some of the pages while I waited. I remembered the day I found my dad's old Nikon 35mm camera and convinced him to let me learn to use it. Naturally, I shied away from writing, so I taught myself to take pictures to help me record my life instead.

I didn't take pictures of people. No landscapes, no whole objects. What I looked for were the small parts of the whole that made a thing special. The pictures in my book were all about textures. Each one of the textures reminded me of a happy time or place.

As I thumbed through the pages, the memories came back like crocuses in the spring, popping up here and there, unexpected. On one page was the ice from the pond where we went skating. I had loved the way the sunlight caught the bubbles and stress cracks under the surface, as if to show that it was the imperfections that made the ice beautiful. On another page, splotches of rust on the metal sliding door in the shed looked to me like a map of miniature continents. Mom used to let us help her pot flowers back there. I even had a photo of the drops of water on the leaves of one of her transplanted perennials.

Small thumbnail glimpses were all I could afford growing up. The bigger picture often wasn't as attractive. I used to believe I had tiny glimpses of beauty inside of me as well, that if someone ever cared enough to look closely, they would be able to see beyond the weird moments and strange behavior and just see me.

"Hey, Ash?"

My head jerked up and I slapped the book closed. Here I'd been waiting for my dad to surface and I hadn't even heard the office door. He stood by the kitchen table, prying the back off his BlackBerry. I covered my journal with my arm. "Yeah?"

"Did you pick up that battery I asked for? This thing's gone completely dead."

"Yes." I pointed. "It's right over there on the counter, behind the rooster."

He frowned and gave the counter half a glance. "I didn't see it and I've got a conference call in four minutes."

"Hold on." I slipped my journal beneath a pile of magazines on the ottoman and hurried over to help him look. Of course it was there, right where I told him it was. "Hey," I said as I handed it to him, "I was wondering where—"

"Huh." He didn't seem to hear me. "I thought the box would be larger." He ripped open the package—shredded it, was more like it—and pulled out the battery. "They didn't charge you for it, right? It's supposed to be covered in the replacement warranty."

"No, they didn't charge me." I gathered bits of cardboard and plastic he left on the counter and threw them in the trash.

He snapped his new battery into place. "So," he said without looking up. "How's school?"

I waited as he tested his BlackBerry, pressing a series of random buttons before he finally glanced up at me, waiting for an answer. "It's fine," I said.

He nodded and turned his attention back to the phone. "I better not have to reprogram this thing," he muttered, scrolling through his contacts. "How's practice? How're you doing on your time?"

"Good. But listen, I need to find—"

"Oh." He turned the phone so I could see the screen. "Did you put this date on the calendar? I'll be in Houston on Monday. Flight out early Monday morning."

I took a deep breath and let it out slowly. "Yeah, I got it."

"Good."

I watched him fidget with his phone for a few seconds more. Did he know I wanted to ask him about Kyra? Is that why he kept interrupting me? We never spoke about her leaving. We never spoke about anything unpleasant. Well, okay, we never spoke, but if there was even the slightest chance that he knew where she might have gone, I had to ask. "Dad, I need to know. Did Kyra ever tell you—"

His phone rang and he held up a finger to me. "Hold on," he mouthed, and pressed the BlackBerry to his ear. "Don. Hello. Yes, now's perfect. Everyone on the line? Great." He walked back to his office as he was talking. "All right," he said. "Let's get started."

Then he closed the door.

I searched through the rest of our bedroom that evening, but I never found anything that even hinted where Kyra could have gone. While Dad was in his office, I searched through the kitchen drawers. I poked around the great room. Nothing. It was like Kyra had simply walked out the door that day and disappeared.

I waited to ask Dad again, but he was on his conference call for hours and when he emerged from his office, he was already on the phone again. I tried to pass him a note, but he gave me a helpless shrug and mouthed, "We'll talk later."

I smiled at him and nodded, even though I knew we never would.

When I felt my way into the kitchen the next morning, Dad was standing by the sink, eating scrambled eggs straight from a frying pan.

I squinted against the sunlight slashing in through the windows. "You want me to get a plate for you?"

"Thanks, I'm almost done." He scooped up another bite. "Do you want—" When he turned to talk to me, he stopped the fork halfway to his mouth. "Ooop. Are you feeling okay?"

"I'm fine," I grabbed a couple of aspirin and poured myself a glass of orange juice. He'd left the carton on the counter—along with the eggshells and a drippy whisk he must have used for the eggs. Mom would have had a fit. I wondered sometimes if she had always cleaned up after him and we never noticed or if he had been more careful when she was around. I ripped a paper towel from the roll to wipe it up. "Didn't sleep well last night," I said.

"Ah." He set the pan in the sink and filled it up with water. "Hate it when that happens."

"So do I." I tossed back the aspirin and washed it down with the orange juice. "Blegh. I just brushed my teeth."

"Hate that even worse," he said.

"So do I." I wadded up the sticky paper towel and threw it in the trash as I started to shuffle back toward my room. In the hallway I turned back, but he had already moved on to the couch and the Sunday paper, leaving the pan in the sink. We both knew I would come in and clean it up later and I wouldn't say anything to him about it. That was our dance—move throughout the day, don't rock the boat, don't look at anything too closely.

Only I couldn't do the dance anymore. I needed answers more than I needed to hide from the confrontation. I walked back toward the great room, took a deep breath, and jumped out of the safety zone. "Actually, I didn't sleep at all last night," I blurted. "I was thinking about Kyra. Wondering how she's doing."

Dad glanced up slowly from his paper, and for an excruciating moment I thought he was going to follow my lead. "You know Kyra," he said finally. "I'm sure she's fine." And then he turned the page and went back to reading.

"Dad," I said evenly. "Do you know where she is?"

This time he didn't even look up. "I think," he said, "that she wants to take some time to herself. We need to respect that."

And by "we" he meant *me*. "You didn't answer my question," I said.

"You didn't expect me to."

"Dad, please. I need to talk to her. It's important."

He folded his paper carefully. "This has been a very difficult time, Ashlyn." For the first time, he looked me in the eye. "For everyone."

And with that, he retreated to his office. Like always.

"Ashlyn, hellooo." Michelle waved her hand in front of my face. "Where's your head this morning? I know it's Monday, but . . ."

"Huh?" I blinked out of my stupor.

"You almost stepped into that pothole during our run and now you're trying to open the wrong locker."

I looked up at the locker number. "Crud."

"No kidding." She laughed as she left down the hall for class. "Wake up!"

I moved to my own locker, shaking my head. It had been another long night. I couldn't stop thinking of Kyra, trying to remember anything she might have said before she left that would tell me where she was. Dad had been preparing for that sales meeting in Houston. He left for the airport about the time I left to go running. All the while I was waiting, anticipating, dreading the next trance. If I was right about it repeating until it was completed, I could get sucked in at any moment.

AP lang dragged on for what felt like eons that morning. There are just so many essays on culture and anarchy that can be digested before lunch. From the whispers and sounds of fidgeting around me, I could tell I wasn't the only one getting restless waiting for the class period to end.

I sighed and I slouched down in my chair, watching the second hand make a slow sweep of the clock on the wall when the room began to disappear. My head buzzed. Sudden. Intense. Like a live wire had been poked into my skull. And then everything around me faded to black. I squinted desperately at the time on the clock as the light disappeared—9:25—and felt the pinch of my fingers closing around my mechanical pencil.

Rain, black pavement, lights growing brighter, brighter, brighter. Someone is standing in the road. I realize with a start that it's not me. He starts to turn his head. He.

The last detail took me by such complete surprise that it threw me right out of the trance. Ice washed over me as I realized that the trance was *not* a repeat of my own accident. This was something new. Slowly the sounds around me began to register again.

". . . seen it happen before?"

". . . epilepsy."

". . . who to call?"

My eyes fluttered and the black clouds in my vision began to dissolve. Pieces of the room fell into place like a crazy Tetris game. I lifted my head from my desk and tried to focus on the wall of jeans and T-shirts swirling around me.

"Ashlyn?" Ms. Crawley's face came into focus right in front of mine. Her brows were scrunched into a kind of perplexed worry. "Do you know where you are?"

"I'm in class."

"Good. Do you—"

I squinted at my watch. 9:28. Three minutes had passed. "Did I write?"

"What?"

"Write." I grabbed her hand. "Did I write anything?" And then as the dizziness passed enough to focus, I saw the numbers scrawled across my notebook. I ripped out the page and folded it, folded it, folded it, concentrating hard to make each crease, trying not to let the tears surface. What was happening to me?

"Man, she's lost it," someone behind me said. Several other someones laughed.

Ms. Crawley glared at them. "Class, take your seats." To me she said, "Do you think you can stand?"

I nodded, even though the room still felt like it was turning on an unsteady axle.

Riley, the guy who sat across the aisle from me, nudged my arm. "You dropped this." He held out my mechanical pencil.

I recoiled, afraid that by touching it, I could be pulled into the trance again. "It's not mine."

"Yeah it is. It rolled off your desk." He offered it again.

I couldn't move.

"Um, are you going to take it?" Riley reached across the aisle and I leaned away from his outstretched hand.

Ms. Crawley patted my shoulder. "Let's get you to the nurse's office."

"Oh. No." That wouldn't be good. I needed to go someplace where I could be alone while I thought this thing out, not to the nurse's office to be observed. "No. Really, I'm okay. I just need to splash some water on my face or something."

She cocked her head, frowning. "I'd feel better if you saw the nurse."

"It was just . . ." I struggled for the word and lowered my voice. "It was a minor episode. You know, the epilepsy. But I'm fine now."

I could tell by the pinch between her eyes that the lie wasn't going to cut it this time. "This . . . episode was different than any I've seen from you before." She bent down and whispered in my ear, "Sweetie, you were convulsing."

Suddenly, my chest felt too tight. I couldn't breathe. *Convulsions?* I didn't have a quick answer for that.

Ms. Crawley stood. "May I have a volunteer to accompany Ashlyn to the health center?"

Nick Cumberland stood up. "I'll take her."

"No. It's okay," I said quickly. "I can go by myself."

Ms. Crawley ignored me. "Thank you, Nick."

A mixture of anger and humiliation burned in my face. "This isn't necessary," I said as I stuffed the note into my pocket and gathered my books. "I do not need an escort." But Ms. Crawley was already opening her textbook at the front of the class and Nick was waiting by my desk.

"Your pencil," Riley said.

"Keep it," I told him, and allowed Nick to lead me out of the room.

In the hall, Nick seemed to forget how he had ignored me before class the other day and now was the very picture of concern. "Are you sure you're going to be okay?" he asked, circling his arm around my shoulders. "That was really weird."

I shrugged away from him. "Thanks a lot."

He stuffed his hands in his pockets and looked so dejected that I almost felt bad. "I'm serious," he said.

"I'm fine." I wished it were true. As calm as I was trying to appear on the outside, my stomach felt like it had been turned inside out. I may not have been happy about it, but at least when I believed I was reliving my own accident, I could hold on to the idea that there was some logical explanation for the repeat trances. This one proved I was wrong.

"I'm really sorry," Nick said. It took me a second to realize he wasn't talking about what happened in class.

"Don't," I warned.

"I just wanted you to know."

Suddenly, my throat felt achy and tight. "I'm sorry, too," I managed.

Michelle and I huddle in a small alcove under the stairs near the library—about the only space that isn't wall-to-wall people. It's the first time we've been invited to a party with the A-list crowd and we're a little out of our element. At least I am. Michelle's watching them, her eyes as bright as Christmas morning. She points across the room and shouts something to me but I can't hear her over the music, the laughter. I nod just to prove I'm really listening and the next thing I know, she's pulling me into a hug.

"I knew you'd understand," she says, and then she takes off.

From the alcove, I watch her push and weave through the crowd until she's swallowed in the sea of people and I lose her altogether. I hesitate for a moment before stepping out of the shadows myself. I've never been as fearless as Michelle when it comes to navigating the social scene. In fact, I'm scared to death, but it's my first real party and I don't want to spend it on the outside looking in.

I shoulder my way through the crowd, looking for a familiar face. Everyone I recognize from school seems to already be deep in conversation and I don't know how to insert myself into their group.

A few of them glance at me, but not for long. I'm starting to feel really stupid. I'm not one of them. I have no business being here. But just when I'm about to back out of the room, a deep voice says, "Ashley?"

I jump and spin around. Nick Cumberland is standing there, a plastic cup in one hand, the thumb of the other hooked casually through the belt loop on his jeans. My mouth goes dry and I gesture to myself, questioning. He smiles. Yes, he's talking to me.

"Ashlyn," I say.

"What?"

"It's Ashlyn, not Ashley."

He nods slowly like he's weighing the name against his memory. "Right," he agrees. "From chem."

"AP lang," I say softly.

He leans closer and rests his hand on my arm. "What?"

My skin tingles at his touch. I can't speak. I can barely breathe.

His gaze moves beyond me to the crowd around us. "Too loud," he yells.

All I can do is nod, like one of those old bobble-head dolls. He's still talking, but the words are lost to me. I'm too preoccupied watching the curve of his lips, the fringe of his near-black lashes surrounding soft brown eyes.

He pauses and then smiles. "I said, do you want to find someplace quieter to talk?" He's looking straight at me now, those brown eyes laughing.

"Sure." I try to sound casual even though I'm freaking out inside.

He leads the way through the crowd and into the kitchen, pausing long enough to toss his cup and snag a couple of fresh drinks from the counter.

"After you," he says, and gestures at the back door with his head.

Outside, the moon paints soft bars of light through the porch railing and onto a rattan love seat where Nick settles onto the cushion. He looks up at me expectantly and holds out one of the drinks. His fingers touch mine as I take the cup *from his hand, and sparks tingle up my arm.*

When I sit next to him, he flashes his perfect smile at me. "Much better."

He takes a sip of his drink and I automatically raise my cup to do the same. I try to ignore the sour yeast smell and the bitter taste as the beer fizzes over my tongue and down my throat, but I choke on it just a little. He pats me on the back a couple of times. "You okay?"

"Yeah. Sure." I take another long drink to prove it. I must look like such a baby to him. It's so obvious I've never even tasted beer before.

Nick tilts his head back and drains his cup. I do the same and he laughs.

"That's what I'm talking about!"

"Nothing to it." But then before I know what's happening, I let loose a huge, sour-smelling belch. That makes him laugh even harder. He forces out one of his own and even though I don't know why, I start to giggle.

"You're all right," he says, like he's surprised or something.

I bump his arm with my shoulder. "You're not so bad yourself." I think I'm smiling, but my lips feel numb.

Suddenly, he stands up. "Hold on. I'll go get us another."

I watch his back disappear through the kitchen door and I pinch myself to be sure I'm not dreaming. How many years have I wished I could work up the nerve to talk to Nick Cumberland? And here he is. With me.

When he returns, Nick sits even closer to me than before. So close that I can smell the beer on his breath and the spicy soap smell of his skin. It makes my stomach flip and I take a long drink from the cup to calm my nerves. Then another. And another. By the time he tells me how beautiful I look, I'm starting to feel peculiarly warm.

My cup is empty. I stare at the foam clinging to the inside and wonder idly if I should offer to get the next round. But then his fingers close over mine and he takes the cup from me.

The next thing that I know, his other hand is on my thigh. My heart jumps as he leans toward me, eyes half-closed, lips half-open. I practically swoon into the kiss. And then he's pressing me back onto the cushions and his hands seem to be everywhere at once. Stoking my face, weaving through my hair, brushing up under my shirt. His callused skin is at once soft and rough against my stomach. I close my eyes and enjoy the sensation.

"Ashlyn?" a voice says. It sounds far away. I twist my head and there's Michelle standing on the steps

of the porch, arms folded tight across her chest. Her
friend Trey is standing behind her, his hands deep in
the pockets of his jeans. He's staring at the ground,
rocking on his heels like he'd rather be anywhere
else but here.

"Are you ready to go?" Michelle asks.

Nick pushes himself up. "I can take her home."

"I don't think so." Michelle's words are all pointy
and harsh with sharp edges. Nick must feel it, too,
because the next thing I know, he's gone.

Ms. Crawley must have already called down to the nurse's
office, because Mrs. Spinelli was waiting for me when we
got there.

"There you are," she said. "I was getting worried."

"We had to stop for her to catch her breath," Nick said
smoothly. Even after everything that happened, I was
surprised by how easily he could lie.

"I see." Mrs. Spinelli ignored him as she took my
wrist, her fingers cool against my pulse. "Thank you, Mr.
Cumberland. You may go back to class now."

I waited until the door closed behind Nick before
speaking. "I'm fine," I assured her. "It was just a—"

"Shhh." Mrs. Spinelli kept her eyes on her watch for a
few seconds more and then released my wrist. "You gave
your teacher quite a fright, you know."

"I'm sorry."

"No need apologize to me." She nodded toward one of the chairs against the wall. "Sit."

I sat. "It was no big deal," I said.

Again she shushed me. "Eyes up here." She pulled a penlight from her pocket and clicked it on like a mini lightsaber. I blinked against the brief stabs of pain as she shined it into one eye and then the other. Finally, she sat back against her desk, folding her arms and cocking her head. "Now," she said. "Tell me how you're feeling."

I lifted a shoulder. "I feel *fine*." I was lying as easily as Nick now. In reality, I felt weak, dizzy, terrified.

"So you said." Mrs. Spinelli carefully replaced the penlight into her pocket. "Nevertheless, you should go home and rest." When I began to protest, she held up her hand to silence me. "I know. You feel *fine* now. But given your medical history, we want to err on the side of caution. I can call your father for you if you would like."

My chest twisted. She couldn't call my dad; he was out of town and the school district had rules about that sort of thing. If a parent was going to be away, they had to send a note, giving alternate numbers where they could be reached and naming a guardian in case of an emergency.

Dad and I had a silent agreement that we would ignore the note rule. Neither one of us wanted to alert the authorities about how long or how often he was away. It wasn't exactly legal for me to be left alone since I was still a minor, but I didn't want to stay with someone else while he was gone and he didn't want to make the arrangements. Besides, we both knew that some secrets were best kept within the family.

"Um, I think he had a meeting today. He'll be out of the office."

"No problem." She scanned the emergency contact card we'd had to fill out at the beginning of the year. "We'll call his cell."

Even though I guessed he wouldn't answer if he saw the school's number on his caller ID, my palms turned clammy as she dialed the phone. I shouldn't have worried. He'd had more than his share of calls from school nurses. Why should he interrupt his day and race to the school only to find that nothing was wrong? Nothing he could fix, anyway. It was easier for him to just let the situation work itself out.

Mrs. Spinelli tried him twice and got his voice mail each time.

"I tell you what," she said finally. "You go ahead and lie down on one of the cots and I'll keep trying to reach him." She started punching the numbers on her phone again.

"I seriously don't need to lie down. Besides, I have a test in trig next period that I can't miss and—"

She didn't even glance up. "We'll give your teacher a note."

I was starting to get desperate. "You don't understand. If I miss classes I can't go to track practice and we have a big meet com—"

She shook her head. "Hon, we can't clear you to participate in school athletics again until we have a note from your doctor."

"What? You can't be serious." What was I going to tell Dad about *that*? "There is nothing wrong with me."

"School policy," she said firmly. "I'm going to need you to lie down until I reach your father."

She directed me to one of the narrow beds at the back of the room, where I sank onto the edge of the mattress, defeated. I silently watched her pull the thin curtain along its ceiling track to surround me. The rubber soles of her shoes squeaked over the tiles as she walked back over to her desk, leaving me alone. Which is what I wanted in the first place.

Her chair creaked, the legs scraping against the floor as she must have scooted herself close to her desk. A moment later, I could hear the soft rustle of paper. I was already forgotten.

I wished I could forget as easily. This latest trance had me rattled. Over the years, I'd never embraced the trances, but I had learned to live with them once I knew what to expect. But this one was different. Stronger. According to Ms. Crawley, I hadn't just been zoned out and writing while I was in the trance. I'd been *convulsing*.

I hugged my arms and tried not to think about the guy in the road, or the lights racing toward him. With a sick feeling in my stomach I wondered if that guy could be Nick. It was right after I saw him at the mall that the first trance had sucked me in. This one happened while we were in the same classroom. Maybe seeing him was some kind of trigger. Except that had never happened before. But then, things had changed since the accident, hadn't they?

Again I thought of Kyra. Was she seeing the vision, too? What details could she see that I was missing? If I was meant to warn Nick, I had to find out what was in her vision so I would know what to tell him.

But first, I would have to find her, and I didn't know how to do that. The whole situation left me feeling weary and defeated.

I stretched out on the bed, the mattress rustling like a potato chip bag with every movement. It must have been covered in plastic under the sheets—I didn't want to think why. The pillow was like a rock beneath my head, the starched pillowcase coarse and stiff against my cheek. Still, I closed my eyes, only half-listening to Mrs. Spinelli confer with the office about what to do with me.

". . . father is unreachable . . . That's right. Ashlyn Greenfield. Yes, she's the one. Terrible, wasn't it. . . . Well, there's the problem. According to the file, we need his authorization to take her off school property or to seek medical . . . well, of course I tried his cell, but he didn't answer. . . . I left a message. . . . Right. . . . I can just . . ."

My head buzzed and my mind began to drift into gray static. Mrs. Spinelli's words kept playing like a looped tape in my head. "She's the one. Terrible. Terrible. Terrible."

10

Behind my closed eyelids, I saw a replay of my dad's non-reaction when I had asked about Kyra the day before. *She needs some time to herself*, he had said. Which only confirmed that he knew where she was. The ache in my chest dug deeper. Why would he want to keep that from me? Or was she the one who wanted the keeping? Either way, it made me want to curl up in a ball and cry, but that wouldn't do me any good. Crying wouldn't stop the trances.

I thought of Dad locking himself in his office whenever he was home and I wondered what else he was hiding from me. And then my breath caught. I bolted up on the cot. Dad didn't have to tell me where Kyra went. He was a businessman. He kept records. There had to be something in his office that would point me in the right direction. I just had to get home to find it.

***

Mrs. Spinelli and her squeaky shoes stepped out into the hall about a quarter after ten. I didn't move for a full minute after that, just to be sure. The room sounded empty. It *felt* empty. I pulled back the corner of the curtain to peek out. She was gone.

Just then the class bell rang and the hall filled with students. I slipped out into the crush of them and grabbed my backpack from my locker. A lot of the seniors left school for the day after fourth period, so I just walked out with them.

If anyone at school asked what happened to me, I could always say my dad had sent someone to pick me up. When he got home that night, I'd have him write a note to that effect. Or more to the point, I would type it up for him and have him sign it. Chances were he wouldn't even read it. He hardly ever read school papers. That had always been my mom's department.

And now it was mine.

Even though I knew Dad was in Houston, I hesitated outside his office door. The office was like his inner sanctum. I almost felt bad for violating it, but the need to find Kyra outweighed my respect for his privacy.

I started with the desk drawers, pulling the wide middle one out slowly, tentatively. Everything in the drawer was laid out in precise, meticulous order—envelopes and Post-it pads lined up at right angles, pens all facing the same direction, even the paper clips were nestled in uniform rows. That kind of organization seemed strange for someone who couldn't remember to put the cap back on the milk or put away his own laundry. But I'd been through enough therapy sessions to guess the reason why. It was a compulsive thing. In the house, the office was his refuge. Here, he was master. Outside the office doors he had no control.

I closed the drawer, feeling more than a little bit sad as I moved on to the smaller side drawers. Everywhere I looked, it was the same: papers, notebooks, files all painstakingly placed. I sifted through them gingerly, careful not to disturb the order.

I found it in the credenza. Almost passed over it, as a matter of fact. At first when I saw the unfamiliar credit card statement, I figured it was for Dad's business account, but instead of BG Consulting, the card was issued to Benjamin Greenfield. A personal account—unusual because I'd been paying all the household bills and this credit card wasn't one of them.

I pulled the file from the drawer and laid it on the desk, opening it carefully like it might self-destruct. There weren't many charges on the card, so the fee for a prepaid cell phone stood out. Holding my breath, I thumbed through several months' worth of credit card bills. Sure enough, the charges started the second week in February, the week that Kyra had moved away.

Hands trembling now, I turned back to the desk and searched through the files for Gamut Prepaid Cellular. It was tucked into a folder marked, simply, *K*. I laid that file on top of the credit card file and read through the billing information until I found the prepaid phone's number. I copied it onto one of the Post-it notes and carefully put both files away.

My heart hammered inside my chest. This was it. I'd found her. I reached for the phone on the desk, but it felt wrong to call her from there. I stuck the Post-it to the back of my hand, checked to make sure I had left everything in my dad's office in order, and hurried down the hall to my bedroom.

Trembling, I sat at my desk and dialed the phone.

Kyra answered after the second ring. "Dad?"

My heart tumbled. What was this—their private line? Why did they think they had to hide it from me? "Kyra?"

She was quiet for a moment. "Ashlyn?"

"Yeah. It's me."

"How did you get this number?"

"From Dad." Then I corrected myself in a small voice. "From Dad's office."

More silence. "What do you want?"

Her hesitation settled like a weight on my chest. "I . . . I need to talk to you. Can we meet somewhere?"

"No," she said sharply. "We can't."

I wanted to cry. "I need your help."

Silence.

"I keep having trances," I said, pressing on.

"I'm going to hang up."

"No! Please don't. Please. I need—"

"I can't help you, Ashlyn."

I gripped the phone with both hands, wanting to hold on to her, to make her understand. "I need to know what you're seeing, Kyra."

"I don't know what you're talking about."

It was a lie. I knew lying; it was what I did. I recognized it in her voice.

"Kyra, please. I just want the visions to stop."

"So do I," she said quietly.

"Then please help."

"I can't do that." Her voice sounded tired.

"Please, Kyra. I don't know what else to do. I *need* you. You have to help me."

"Like *you* helped *me* before the accident?"

My heart plummeted. *Kyra standing by my bed. Shaking. Scared.*

"I didn't know," I whispered. "Believe me, Kyra, if I'd have known, I would have tried to—"

"It's too late," Kyra said. "We can't go back."

"I didn't know," I said again.

"It's done, Ashlyn. She's gone."

I dropped my head into my hand, tears clinging to my

eyelashes before dripping down onto the Post-it note, smearing her number. "If we can make things right this time—"

"Don't call me again," she said, and hung up.

I held the phone to my ear until I heard the dial tone. Then the beeping. Then the automated voice, "If you would like to make a call, please hang up and try again." Letting the phone clatter onto the desk, I hugged my arms. "I'm sorry," I whispered to the emptiness around me. "I'm so sorry."

It's the morning after the party and I can't think straight. It feels like my skull split apart and the two halves are grinding together. My mouth tastes like a sewer.

"Ashlyn . . ."

"Not now." I roll out of the bed and lurch to the bathroom to puke.

An hour later I'm dressed, hunched over the kitchen table. One hand massages my temples and the other holds a cup of steaming herbal tea. Mom is humming off-key in the other room. Kyra slides into the chair next to mine.

"I have to know." Her voice is low and conspiratorial. "It's important. My half of the puzzle . . ." She's unfolding a sheet of paper in front of me. I can't focus on the numbers.

"What is this?"

"It's the numbers," she whispers. "I need to know what yours says, what you saw. I'm afraid that . . ." Her voice cracks and she glances toward the other room, where the awful humming is coming from. "I think something's going to happen to—"

I push her paper away. "It didn't come to me."

"What?"

With some effort, I stand, swaying a little. I grab the table for support. My head's still throbbing and the movement isn't helping any. "I haven't written anything for over a week," I say. "Whatever this is, it's just you. It doesn't mean anything."

She pushes back from the table, knocking her chair over. It clatters to the floor and the noise hammers straight into my brain. I groan.

"Look at you," she hisses. "You can't even stand on your own feet!"

I turn from her, which only causes the room to spin.

"You didn't write because you're drunk." Kyra spits out the words like they've been dipped in poison.

"I'm not drunk," I say. Not anymore. But I keep that part to myself.

"Then it's not too late," she persists. "Maybe you haven't gotten it yet. Maybe you just need to—"

"What I need," I say, "is to lie down." I walk away.

When I wake, long shadows fill my room. Tentatively, I raise my head and look at the clock.

"Crud!"

I throw back the covers and jump from the bed. The mall will be closing in less than an hour and I need to get a new lens kit. The old lens has a hairline crack in it and I want to take pictures on our Spanish class trip to the museum on Monday. I brush my teeth and splash water on my face and then go looking for Mom, pulling my hair back into a sloppy ponytail as I go.

"You're up," she says when she sees me.

"The mall closes in forty-five minutes," I snap. "Why didn't you wake me?"

"I thought maybe you didn't feel up to going." She's looking at me in a funny way that makes me think maybe Kyra told her about me drinking.

"I need to get the lens kit." My voice comes out harsher than I intended and I feel a little guilty, but my irritation won't let me back down.

"It's getting late . . ."

"I can go by myself if you don't want to—"

"Oh, no you don't." She's already standing up and grabbing her car keys. "Rules are rules."

I take the keys, muttering about how stupid it is that I need to have another driver in the car when I've had my license for three weeks. Mom just

*ignores me. All the way to the mall, she pretends like
I wasn't just a complete troll to her. I'm not in the
mood for her forced cheerfulness, but I don't really
want to hold on to my foul mood, either.*

*I let my mind wander back to last night's party,
out on the porch with Nick Cumberland. My stomach
flips as I remember how he kissed me. I raise my
fingers to my lips.*

"Both hands on the wheel," Mom says.

*I can't stop reliving the memories as we walk
through the mall. It doesn't seem real. Me and Nick
Cumberland! I know I'm grinning like an idiot,
but I can't help myself. I've had a crush on Nick
since seventh grade when our class was playing
dodgeball in gym. I caught a hard throw by Scott
Gardener and stood there, dazed. Nick smiled at me
and said, "Nice catch, Greenfield." Until that moment, I didn't think he even knew I existed, but he
said my name! The fact that he hardly spoke two
words to me from that moment on never swayed my
devotion to him. And now we're together! It's like a
dream.*

*I'm so besotted that I don't even mind when my
mom says she needs to stop into Jo-Ann to get some
fabric for new pillows in the study. She makes her
purchase and we're on the way down to Camera*

Corner when I see him sitting by the fountain in the mall's center court.

My heart leaps as I recognize Nick's tousled brown hair and his Springfield High jersey. But just as quickly, I see that he's not alone and the breath goes out of me. Alicia Hayes is sitting on his lap, her face all smashed up against his. His hand is splayed across her backside, thumb tucked inside the waistband of her jeans.

My feet stop working and the bile rises in my throat. All I can do is stand there, staring at them. And then Nick looks up, like I've just called his name or something. His eyes meet mine and I watch it register on his face as he remembers last night. His lips part like he's going to say something, but then Alicia pulls him close to her again.

Mom tugs on my arm. "Mall's closing in five minutes," she says. "We'd better hurry if we're going to get that lens kit."

"I want to go home."

"But I thought—"

"I want to go now."

Outside it has started to rain. Mom covers her head with one Jo-Ann bag as we walk to the car and offers another to me, but I don't take it. I don't care if I get soaking wet. I don't care about anything.

We don't talk as we get into the car. Mom tries,

but I couldn't speak even if I wanted to. How could I have been so stupid, thinking last night's make-out meant anything to Nick? He probably knew I'd be an easy target. Naive, inexperienced.

Tears blur my vision and I blink them away. It hurts. It hurts so bad. I drive toward home on autopilot. At the intersection, I pull into the left-hand lane. I watch the light and the oncoming traffic. When it's clear I start the turn.

Then I see the headlights racing toward us.

Mom screams.

And everything goes black.

11

The floor tilted as I stumbled to the bathroom. I barely made it to the toilet and lifted the lid before my stomach heaved. Sweat prickled under my arms and down the length of my spine. I doubled over and threw up again.

Dry heaves gave way to sobs that tore through my chest with a pain I hadn't felt since the accident. I couldn't make them stop. Clothes and all, I climbed into the shower and turned on the spigot. Leaning my forehead against the tiles, I sobbed and hiccuped and let the water wash over me until it ran cold.

Nothing could erase the image of Mom's limp hand on mine. My stomach heaved again, but there was nothing left for me to throw up.

I peeled off my wet clothes, leaving them in a soggy heap on the floor of my bathroom. Even though it was barely past noon, I pulled on my pajamas without even drying myself off completely. Shivering, I hugged my arms, wishing I could make it all go away.

Then my eyes dropped to the vanity drawer. I yanked it open and rummaged through makeup brushes, powder, and tubes of mascara to find the little amber prescription bottle I tossed in there when I got back from the hospital. There were still about a dozen Vicodin left—more than enough to make me go numb. I scooped up the bottle and carried it into my room.

Dropping onto the desk chair, I wrestled with the bottle. Since I couldn't stop myself from shivering, I wasn't having much luck with the childproof lid. Finally, I managed to get it open, but spilled the pills across the desk in the process. I grabbed two of them—twice my prescribed dosage—and stuck them on the back of my tongue. They trailed down my throat like dual hot pebbles when I swallowed. I left the rest of the pills where they lay and crawled into bed, burrowed under the blankets, and tried to forget.

Michelle came over around six. When I didn't get up to answer the door, she snuck around the side of the house and tapped on my bedroom window. I squinted out of my blanket cocoon to see her, hands cupped around her eyes, peering into my room. She saw me and tapped again.

"Let me in," she called.

My head felt like it was filled with helium as I stood up. I wobbled to the window and failed twice before I was able to undo the latch and slide the sash up to let her crawl through.

She didn't even wait until she was all the way inside before she started with the questions. "What's going on? I heard you passed out this morning in school. Are you okay? Why didn't you text me?"

I sank back onto my mattress. "S'no bigdeal." I slurred. "Ahmfine."

"Really." She gave me the up and down. "You look like hell."

I hunched my shoulders. It took a lot more effort than it should have.

She dropped onto Kyra's bed and drew up her feet so that she was sitting cross-legged. Just like Kyra used to do. "So what happened in lang? Are you sick? Was it a seizure?"

I sagged onto the pillows. "It was nothing."

"But why didn't you tell me?" she persisted. "I had to hear about it from Melody Newey in the hall."

"Sorry . . ."

"Well, just don't let it happen again." She laughed and moved on to the next subject, running through the list of the day, checking off each event. "And then guess who I saw when I was at the mall? That cute music-store guy. He told me to tell you hi."

I immediately pictured Jake, his smiling green eyes, his

hand as it reached out for mine. What would he think if he knew about me? What would he say if he saw me now?

"Lynnie? Hello!" Michelle snapped her fingers. "Are you all right?" Her voice sounded far away. "I asked you if you were going to—"

And then she stopped and her eyes went to the desk. I followed her gaze even though I already knew what I would see—the bottle tipped on its side, pills scattered around it like a spotted halo. She stood slowly and walked over to examine them closer. "What's this?"

As much as I wanted to offer her an explanation, my head was too fuzzy to come up with a plausible lie and I knew she wouldn't want to know the truth.

"What *is* this, Lynnie?" Michelle said again. She picked up one of the pills like it was a rat dropping and examined the imprinted code.

"I don't feel well," I said simply.

"What's going *on*?"

Too much. I wouldn't know where to begin. I shook my head.

"Help me understand. Because I have to tell you, this doesn't look good."

"They're prescription."

"I can see that. But why? What's wrong?"

"My . . . back. The accident."

She sat on the bed next to me. "Lynnie, you were done with physical therapy weeks ago." Her voice took on that explaining-something-to-a-small-child tone. "Shouldn't you be off of them by now? Pain pills can become addictive."

"Ahmfine."

"Fine? You're so stoned you can't even talk straight. Is that what was wrong with you at the mall the other night? And in class this morning?"

"I'm . . . not stoned."

She shook her head. "Have you *seen* yourself? You're seriously wasted."

Sure, that's what it must look like through her eyes. My hair hung in a stringy, tangled mess—a result of not drying it before I climbed into bed. I could barely sit up straight. My mascara was probably smudged all over. And I guessed from the way they stung that my eyes were seriously bloodshot. But I wasn't wasted in the classical sense. All I needed was to sleep it off. That's all I *wanted* to do. I lay back down on my pillow again and let my eyes drift shut.

"That's it." I felt the mattress shift as she stood up. "These things are gone." I could hear her sweeping the pills across the desk. Heard her footsteps thud toward the bathroom. Heard the toilet flush.

I pried one eye open. "Michelle . . ."

She was by the bed then, pulling back the covers, yanking on my arms. "C'mon. In the shower. We need to get you sobered up."

I wrenched my arm out of her grasp with more force than I had intended and she stumbled backward a couple of steps. The wounded look on her face twisted like a knife in my gut. "I . . . can do it," I said. "Thanks."

She managed to rearrange her expression so that it was almost a smile. "I'll make you something to eat."

"Thanks," I murmured again. Eating was the last thing I wanted to do, but I wasn't going to argue with her if it would keep her busy. She wouldn't leave the room until I got up, though, so I pushed off the bed and staggered into the bathroom.

I took a real shower this time, scrubbing my hair and scouring my skin with the loofah until it was angry and red. When I was dressed, I padded out into the kitchen, where Michelle had made scrambled eggs and toast.

"I didn't know what you could eat, but I figured you should have some protein in you," she said.

"This is great, thank you." I sat at the table and she put a plate of food in front of me. The smell of the eggs made my stomach sour.

Michelle scraped a chair next to mine and sat. "Is this because your dad is gone so much?" she asked.

My mouth fell open and I stared at her. "Those pills have nothing to do with my dad."

"I'm sorry. I didn't mean to say . . ." She took a deep breath and started again. "I'm just looking for a way to understand. I mean, if it's hard being alone, you could always come hang out at my house when he's gone. . . ."

I speared a bite of eggs angrily and choked them down

to keep from saying anything. She had no idea how wrong she was.

"You remember my aunt Tricia?" she said. "The chiropractor? She works with a lot of whiplash patients and she said it's really common to get hooked on pain medication, so you shouldn't feel too bad. The important thing is to get off of them."

I set my fork down with a clatter. "I am not hooked."

"Good." She smiled at me like I was a three-year-old. "That'll make it easier to give them up."

I pushed back from the table. "Wow."

"I just want to help," she said.

"Then leave," I snapped, "because I really don't need this right now."

She looked at me like I'd just smacked her across the face and I wished I could reel my words back in. I sighed and reached for her. "Michelle, I'm sorry. I've just had a really bad—"

"I should go." She pushed away and stomped from the room. The front door slammed and I felt the concussion deep in my gut.

Dad got home around eleven. By then I had cleaned up the wet clothes in the bathroom, made my bed, and gotten dressed. I had just about finished my homework when I heard the garage door opener crank into life. I quickly checked my room to make sure nothing was out of place.

All I had left to do was to sit at my desk with my books appropriately spread about and wait.

I heard the familiar sound of him filling the house with his presence again—his keys jangling into the Italian ceramic bowl on the end of the counter, his briefcase hitting the kitchen floor with a *thunk*, the creak of the closet door where he would be hanging up his suit coat, his footsteps in the hall coming toward my room.

He swung open the door and I expected his usual, "Hey, Ash. I'm home." Instead he said, "What's this about you skipping school?"

So instead of my usual, "Welcome back," I said, "Huh?"

He took a couple more steps into my room. "School, Ashlyn. I got a call from Mrs. Briggs. She said she saw you coming home midday today, so I checked my voice mail and I had a message from the school *and* from your coach saying the same thing. Are you sick?"

Perfect. Leave it to Mrs. Briggs. "Oh, yeah. I—"

"So it's true?"

My voice shrank. "I wasn't feeling good."

"You weren't feeling *well*."

"That either."

He didn't even smile. "You need to call me if you're going to miss school. I shouldn't be hearing about it second-hand."

"I'm sorry," I murmured.

"I need to be able to count on you, Ashlyn," he said.

"With your mom gone . . ." He let the lecture die there. We both knew it by heart. With Mom gone, I needed to be dependable. Pitch in. Help out. And I did try. I took over the jobs Mom always did, like pay all the bills and organize his travel. I made sure the checkbook was balanced and there was food in the fridge. I did everything I could do so that my dad wouldn't have to worry—which was one reason I didn't demand right then that he explain to me why he had never told me where Kyra was.

"I'll need a note tomorrow," I said softly, and we let it go at that.

The sky outside my window was still on the purple side of pink when I got up the next morning. I washed my face and brushed my teeth, not knowing if Michelle would even show up for our morning run. I had sent her a text to apologize for the day before, but she never responded.

I knew I probably wouldn't be much good to her as a running partner anyway; I was still pretty shaken about the phone call with Kyra. Still, I hoped she would want to stick with the routine. There were so few things left I could count on; I didn't want to lose this, too.

I waited out front, stretching and warming up, for at least fifteen minutes past our appointed meeting time, but she didn't show, so I set off on my own. The first couple of blocks weren't that bad since we never talked at the beginning of the run anyway, but by about half a mile in I realized that it wasn't so much the running I had wanted to hang on to; it was the conversation. Already I missed it. I missed Michelle. But I missed a lot of other things in my life, too, and moping about them was not going to bring them back.

My feet hit the pavement in a quicker cadence. So I was on my own; that was nothing new. By now I should be used to it.

I admit I was feeling rather sorry for myself—which, I can tell you from experience, is never a good thing. All it does is make you more miserable than you already are. It's just that I couldn't help but feel abandoned. I didn't have anyone to turn to who really understood what I was going through. Not just that morning, but as a running theme for my life. My mom was gone. My sister had left and wouldn't even speak to me. From the time I was a little kid, none of my friends stuck around once they discovered what a freak I was. Except Michelle, and now she was gone, too.

I was so absorbed in my self-pity that I didn't realize how far I'd run until I passed the front gates to the Bristol Commons subdivision, which was well past our halfway point. I had just turned around to go back when I heard a woman's voice yell, "No! Bad! Get back here!"

If that wasn't surprising enough, all of a sudden there was a little dog practically under my feet. It was one of those little yip-yip things that looked like a hairy rat—a miniature ball of energy and indignation—yapping and nipping at my ankles. I danced to the side to keep from tripping over it.

The woman raced over and scooped up the dog. "Bad boy, Brutus!" And then to me, "I'm so sorry about that."

Brutus? No wonder the little rat was so indignant. He trembled in her arms, staring me down from underneath his stringy hair. "It's okay," I said. "No harm do—"

"Excuse me," she interrupted, "but don't I know you?"

I squinted at her, but she was backlit by the morning sun so I couldn't really see much beyond her hair rollers and her fuzzy robe. "I don't think—"

"Yes." She took a step closer and Brutus growled. "I know you; you're Ben and Margaret's girl."

My heart clenched at the mention of my mom's name. "I'm sorry, I—"

She gestured to herself with her free hand. "Sister Eaton. From church. You probably don't recognize me without my makeup." She batted her eyelashes and laughed . . . until she remembered, and then her face went white. "I'm . . . uh . . . I'm so sorry about your mother."

An icy knife slashed through my chest. This is where I should have murmured my polite thank you and been on my way, but instead I said flatly, "You don't know me."

Her plucked brows creased and she coughed. "Well, it has been a while. Maybe you don't remember. . . ."

But I did remember her. I remembered every long Sunday morning going to church with my mother while Sister

Eaton and the other ladies from my mother's prayer group whispered behind their hands, casting scandalized looks in our direction. I remembered how they gathered forces when Janelle's mom told everyone how Kyra had claimed to see her husband's heart attack before it happened. I remembered how she was the one who convinced my mother that trance writers were like mediums and received messages from dead people. *Mediums*, she said, *were of the devil.* Good little girls did not commune with dead people. I remembered her and another of the ladies stopping by our house to lecture my mother when she finally gave up and stopped dragging us to church.

Yes, I knew Sister Eaton. But that didn't mean she knew me. Not by a long shot.

"Oh. Well . . ." She fidgeted with Brutus's collar, obviously unsure of what to say. "It was nice to see you again."

"I have to go," I said, and turned away.

"Tell your father I said hello," she called after me.

I just ran. I ran until my thighs ached and my lungs grew hot and tight. It was no use. I could try to forget who I was, but I would never outrun it.

12

Dad was still asleep when I got home. His snores rumbled down the hall in a steady rhythm. I considered
waking him—he had a flight at ten—but I didn't want a
repeat of the tension from the night before. Besides, he
didn't have to be to the airport for another couple of hours
and he'd already signed my note for school, so I tiptoed
past his room and let him sleep.

I did a lot of that, I realized—a lot of tiptoeing around Dad.
It just seemed easier that way. Neither one of us wanted to
look too closely at what had happened. But neither one of
us seemed to be able to move past it, either.

I got ready quietly so I wouldn't disturb him and then
slipped out the door to walk to school.

"What do you think you're doing?" Michelle rolled

alongside me in her car, leaning over to yell at me through the passenger window.

I shaded the sun from my eyes. "I'm walking to school."

"Get in here." She stopped and tried to push the door open, but she couldn't reach far enough to get the momentum she needed, so it kept opening just a few inches before closing again.

"You're talking to me, then?"

"Of *course* I'm talking to you. What kind of question is that?"

A silver Honda rolled up behind Michelle's car and honked.

"Get in!" she yelled again.

I slid into the passenger seat and she stepped on the gas before I had even shut the door.

"What did you mean, am I talking to you?" she asked, sliding me a quick glare. "*You're* the one who's not talking to *me*."

"What? I texted you yesterday and you never texted back. And you didn't come running this morning."

She pursed her lips. "Well, my phone died, so I never got your text."

I ran my finger along the stitching on my backpack. "Oh."

"I didn't mean to be so harsh yesterday," she said.

I glanced over at her. She actually had tears in her eyes. "I appreciate you looking out for me," I told her.

She managed a smile. "It's got to be hard," she said, "but I know you can get through this."

I just nodded and stared out the window. She meant without the meds, of course. I wasn't going to correct her.

All day at school, I couldn't stop thinking about my phone call with Kyra. It got so I couldn't concentrate on anything else. I went through my classes on remote, there but not there. With each passing hour, the walls around me seemed to get tighter and tighter.

By the end of the day, I couldn't bear to be stuck inside any longer. I needed to clear my head. Finally, in my last class, Spanish, I just picked up my books and left. No, that's not exactly accurate; I told Señora Rodriguez that I had to use the restroom and then I just never returned to class.

Instead, I went straight to the locker room and changed into my running gear and walked out to the track. The seventh-period P.E. class was still out on the football field playing some watered-down form of lacrosse, but no one questioned me as I began my warm-ups. That's usually how it happens; if you pretend like you're where you're supposed to be, people tend to leave you alone.

I kept running when they finished their game and wandered off the field, running when the bell rang, running when my teammates started trickling out to the field after school for conditioning. If I couldn't outrun the sting of her rejection, at least I wanted to sweat it out of my system. By the time the rest of the team started to trickle out to the track, my legs were numb and my chest was on fire, but I kept going.

Michelle jogged up beside me on the track. "You didn't wait for me!"

I spared her a glance and then focused on the track again. "I'm sorry," I puffed. "Got. Out. Early."

"Whoa," she said. "You'd better take it down a notch. You're sounding winded."

"I'm fine," I said automatically.

"So what are you doing tonight? Trey and some of the guys are having movie night at his house and they invited us to come."

"I have . . . to work," I wheezed.

"Oh." She looked like she was going to pout for a second and then her face brightened. "Ooh. Then you can see that cute music-store guy."

I shot her a sideways glance. I don't know why it bugged me that she never seemed to be able to remember his name, but it did. "Jake," I corrected.

"That's him. I do like that boy."

I slowed to a walk and she slowed with me. "No," I rasped. "Go. On." She pulled ahead with a steady stride.

That's when Coach Mendenhall blew his whistle and gathered the team by the pole-vaulting mats. He gave some instructions for the day's drills and then he released everyone . . . except me.

"Greenfield? Could I speak with you for a moment?"

Just the tone of his voice was enough to make my stomach sink. "Yes?"

He waited until everyone else had cleared out of earshot, then he tucked his clipboard up under his arm. "I spoke with Mrs. Spinelli today."

"Oh."

"You shouldn't be here, should you? Why didn't you tell me about your mishap yesterday?"

"It wasn't a mishap," I protested. "I'm perfectly fine."

"So you have your doctor's note?"

"Just one from my dad."

He shook his head. "You know the rules, Greenfield. I appreciate your dedication, but we have to follow procedure. Bring in a doctor's note and then we'll talk."

"But the meet."

"You'll have to miss it. That gives you all of spring break to get your paperwork together." He must have read the disappointment on my face because his tone softened. "It might do you well to take some time off. I appreciate how hard you've been working to get your strength back, but we don't want to push you *too* hard."

"No! I—"

He shook his head. "No arguing. Don't come back without the note."

***

I was still angry as I stuffed my clothes into the washer later that afternoon. Angry at Mrs. Spinelli for butting her nose into practice. Angry at Coach Mendenhall for sitting me out two days before the meet. Angry at myself for not figuring out where I was going to get a doctor's note.

Maybe I should have told Dad, but he wasn't going to spend good money for some doctor to tell him I was fine. I'd figure out the note. I just didn't know how.

I grabbed my wet clothes from the day before and started to turn out the pockets before sticking the pants in the washer. The folded-up piece of paper from AP lang fell out from one of them. My breath caught and I grabbed it off the floor. I abandoned the washer and took the note into the family room, sitting down on the couch before I carefully unfolded the paper. These numbers were written neatly, almost timidly. I dropped my chin onto my hand as I studied them. What did that mean?

The clock in the hall signaled the half hour and I jumped up. "Crud!" If I didn't hurry, I was going to miss the bus to the mall and then I really would be late for work. I folded the note back up and tucked it inside my backpack as I ran out the door.

I dreaded going in to ShutterBugz that night because I didn't want to see Jake. No, that's not completely true. I wanted to see Jake. I just didn't want Jake to see *me*. After how I had freaked out when he took me home on Saturday, I didn't know how to face him. I was only scheduled from six until nine, but three hours was plenty of time to be humiliated.

All the way to the mall, I dared to hope he wasn't working that night, but when I got there, I could hear his music before I had even made it through Nordstrom. My heart sank.

At ShutterBugz, Gina sat on her stool, thumbing through a magazine with a bored expression on her face, just like the first time I met her. When I slid behind the counter, she opened the pages wider so that I could see the strollers and car seats, empty and sterile. A baby catalog.

"You see how much more interesting this stuff would be if they actually stuck a kid in them?" she said. "I mean, they should show them in use, give them some life. These things"—she gestured at the open pages—"I don't feel them at all."

"This one's kind of cute," I said, pointing out a jogging stroller with a little plastic drop-down windshield.

She just *hmmphed* and slapped the magazine shut. "They're all 'cute,'" she said. "That's the problem. I don't need cute, I need . . ." She clapped her hand over her mouth.

I thought she was going to be sick and I didn't know whether to jump out of the way or rush forward to help her. I did neither, but froze where I stood. "What is it?"

"I just about said 'practical,'" she whispered.

"What?"

"Practical. *Practical*. I've turned into my mother!" She dropped the catalog into the garbage can and stood. "That's it. I can't take it anymore." She pulled her bag from under the counter. "I'm out of here."

I took her place on the stool and tried to busy myself with sorting through the day's order forms, but I couldn't help sneaking a peek at the music-store window. Jake was inside, helping a lady and a young boy with some kind of long, silver instrument. I couldn't tell from my vantage point what it was.

I reached for my backpack again and gingerly took the note from the pocket. If I could decipher the numbers, I'd be one step closer to figuring out what the trance was trying to tell me. I'd be one step closer to making it stop.

I spread it open on the counter and stared at the string of numbers.

$$1 + 1 + 2 + 5 = 9$$
$$1 + 5 + 4 + 5 + 2 + 3 + 7 + 5 = 32$$
$$3 + 2 = 5$$

There had to be something in them I was supposed to understand, I just couldn't figure out what it was.

"What'cha looking at?" Gina slipped up behind me. I'd

been so intent on the numbers that I hadn't even heard her there.

I jumped and slapped my hand over the paper. "I thought you went home."

"Can't find my keys." She leaned in as much as her stomach would allow and tried to peek over my shoulder. "What've you got there?"

Closing my fingers around the paper, I turned to face her. "Nothing."

"You should know you're only going to make me more curious by being so secretive. What is it? A love letter?"

"Hardly." I inched my hand behind my back.

She laughed at that. "Don't worry, I'm not going to wrestle you for it." She opened up the drawer beneath the counter and began rooting through the flyers and sales slips. "Where did I put those things?"

I felt more than a little ridiculous for my reaction. It's not like anyone was going to know where the numbers came from. "It's just a note," I offered.

She looked up at me, grinning, and abandoned her search. "From who?"

"No one. I mean . . ." I sighed and uncrinkled the paper. I don't know, maybe in a way I *wanted* to show it to her. Since Kyra wouldn't even speak to me, I had no one to talk to about the numbers. Even if I couldn't tell Gina what they were, at least by letting her see them, I wouldn't feel so alone.

I held out the note to her and she glanced at it quickly. "Well, aren't you full of surprises. I never would have pegged you for being into numerology."

"I—I'm not, really," I stammered.

She held out her hand. "May I?" I handed over the paper to her and she laid it on the counter, smoothing it with her hand. "Whoa. Whose numbers are these?"

I shook my head, looking over *her* shoulder now. "I don't know. Why?"

"Whoever's it is, is in trouble."

My mouth went dry and my lips could barely form the question. "What do you mean?"

She looked at me strangely. "The number vibrations," she said. "These numbers are warnings."

Vibrations. Warnings. I felt like she'd dumped a bucket of ice over me. "You . . . you know how to read these things?"

She shrugged. "I like to dabble."

"Dabble," I repeated. "So you . . . do numerology?"

She straightened and pressed one hand to the small of her back. "Well, I don't *do it* do it. I mean, I'm not a numerologist or anything. I've read a bunch about it, ran my own numbers, that kind of thing."

"Oh," I murmured. "And these numbers are . . . bad?"

"I thought you . . ." She shifted her weight, pushing a strand of hair behind her ear. "How did you say you got this?"

I stared at the writing on the page and debated how to

answer that question. How much *could* I say? "My sister," I began.

Gina cocked her head to the side, eyes never leaving the paper. "Ah. I didn't know you had a sister."

"She moved out a while ago."

She glanced up at me quickly. "Hmmm," she said, and turned her attention back to the paper. "But it's not hers, is it?"

I shrugged. "You . . . you said it was a warning," I said cautiously. I wasn't sure I wanted to go there, but I had to *know*. "How do you see that?"

"Well, first let me sit down. My feet are like water balloons." I moved out of the way and she eased herself up on the stool. "I'm telling you," she grumbled, "this is not what I signed up for when I wanted to have a baby."

"The warning," I reminded her, pointing to the end number of one of the equations. "I thought five was a good number."

She nodded. "It is. Or, it can be. But look at the compound numbers before it. Eleven signals hidden dangers. And twelve, well, that's got victim written all over it right there. And sixteen? That's the tarot association for the Shattered Citadel. It's a signal that a strange fatality awaits. So, like I said—"

"No." I shook my head. "I don't even know what you're talking about with the signals and citadels and everything. I've never heard of any of that."

"Right." She smoothed her hands over her stomach. "Because you're probably used to looking at the Pythagorean System. But the Chaldeans taught that the compound number vibrations were just as important as the single. So if you look at these compounds before you reduce them, you're going to get more insight to add to your reading."

I had no idea what she was talking about. Anyway, Kyra and I already knew that the visions were warnings. What we didn't know was what to do about it. "Can you tell anything else by this? Like who or when? What's going to happen?"

She leaned back, resting her elbow on the counter, and gave me a hard look. "Ashlyn, what is this thing?"

I shook my head. I'd already said too much. "It's nothing," I said, and took the paper back. I folded it carefully and stuck it in my pocket.

Gina watched me for a moment and then shrugged. "Whatever." She lowered herself carefully from the stool. "I gotta get going." She reached into her pocket and then rolled her eyes. "Can you believe this?" she said, holding up her keys. "I had them the whole time."

13

I hoped Jake would be busy all night and would never have the chance to notice I was working. I sure noticed him. I couldn't help myself. No matter how much I tried to pretend I didn't care, I'd find my attention shifting to Kinnear Music. Every time I saw Jake seated at the piano, my breath caught for an instant. I thought of riding on the back of his Indian, my arms wrapped around his waist. My face turned hot at the memory.

The whole mall seemed to be unusually slow that night. I pulled out my homework and lost myself in conjugating the Spanish vowels I should have finished in class. I didn't even notice that someone was standing in front of the kiosk until he cleared his throat.

I glanced up and a warm shiver ran through me. Jake

stood before the counter, holding a little plastic cup in each hand.

"Mango–passion fruit or guava-strawberry?"

"Excuse me?"

He half-shrugged. "They're giving away samples at Smoothie King, so I brought you one."

I couldn't help but smile. "Aw. Thanks. I've never gotten a smoothie from a boy before."

"First time for everything." He held up one of the cups with a flourish. "This one is mango–passion fruit. And this"—he held up the other—"is guava-strawberry. Which one do you want?"

"Uh . . ." I didn't really care. It was enough to know he'd been thinking of me—and apparently not in a bad way. I tried not to smile too big. "I'll try the mango one. Thanks."

"You bet." He handed me the cup.

"Cheers," I said, and we touched cups together. Both of us downed our sample in one swallow.

He threw a quick glance back at the music store. "I guess I should get back to work," he said, but he made no effort to go.

I wondered if I was supposed to say something that would release him. "Um . . ."

"Yeah," he agreed. "Um . . . do you need a ride again tonight? I brought my dad's car this time. Not as loud."

That was even sweeter than the smoothie. Had he

brought his dad's car in anticipation of giving me a ride? "Are you serious?"

"Of course. Well, okay, it could use some muffler work, but *relatively*, it's not that loud."

"No, I mean—" One look at his grin and I could tell he knew exactly what I meant, and for a moment, I actually considered taking the ride. But I couldn't risk him seeing me slip into a trance. He'd think I was a total freak. It was better for me to stay far away from Jake. "I appreciate it," I said, "but I have a ride tonight. Thank you, though."

His smile faltered, but he recovered it quickly. "Well. Good. Some other time, then."

"Thanks for the smoothie." I raised the empty cup and tried to return the smile. I'm not quite sure I succeeded.

"I've got to get back to work," he said again, and this time he hurried back to the music store, dropping his cup into a garbage can along the way.

Michelle was way too perky when we went running the next morning, jabbering on about the movie night at Trey's and our upcoming spring break. "I can't *wait* for South Carolina," she said. "My uncle has a house right on Seabrook Island. It's going to be like eighty-five the whole time we're there. I'm so sick of the rain, aren't you?"

I nodded but tried to concentrate on my stride so I wouldn't have to give her a real answer. Truth was, I wasn't looking forward to spring break. There was nothing to look forward *to*. Dad would be traveling, I would be working. Woo-hoo. To be fair, Michelle had invited me to vacation with her family, but I turned her down, for obvious reasons.

I also couldn't forget what Gina had said about the numbers. *A Shattered Citadel*, she'd said. A strange fatality.

The dark road flashed through my head, the rain, the bright lights, the boy standing there . . .

"I said, I wish you'd come with us," Michelle practically yelled. "Are you even listening?"

"Yeah," I said. "Sorry. Just a little winded."

"We can take it slower," she offered.

Now she thought I was an invalid. I stretched my stride a little longer and picked up the pace. "Not necessary," I said.

She laughed and sped to keep up with me. "Man, we could use you at the meet tomorrow."

I just nodded. I didn't need to be reminded of all the things I was missing.

That afternoon I sat at my desk and tried to concentrate on my homework, but the house was too quiet. I couldn't stand to look at the emptiness where Kyra should have been. I couldn't stand the silence where there should have been conversation.

I wandered aimlessly through the house until I found

myself standing outside Dad's office door, wondering if he might have Kyra's address hidden in there somewhere, like he had the phone number.

No. I turned away. Even if I did find it, how would I get Kyra to talk to me? I'd been slapped down enough. I grabbed my backpack and walked out the front door.

I didn't *plan* on going to the mall so early. It just seemed like the natural place to be, even though I wasn't scheduled to work until five. I hoped Gina would be working. I wanted to talk to her some more about the numbers.

When I got to ShutterBugz, the Be Back sign was sitting on the counter. I figured maybe Gina was on break, so I wandered over to the food court, hoping I would find her there. Sure enough, I found her sitting at one of the back tables with her feet propped up, eating bourbon chicken.

"Hey!" she called when she saw me. "What are you doing here so early?"

I shrugged. "I have some . . . shopping to do and I saw you sitting here, so . . ."

She pushed a chair toward me with her foot. "Join me. Take a load off."

I dropped my backpack onto an empty chair and sat on the one she offered me.

"Don't you want to get something to eat?" she asked.

I shook my head. "No. I ate before I came."

"So," she said, smoothing her shirt over her belly. "What's up?"

I hesitated for a moment. Suddenly, I felt foolish for what I was about to ask her. She watched me expectantly, waiting, and I let it tumble out. "I . . . I was curious about that numerology system you were telling me about."

Her smile was instantaneous. "Sure. What do you need to know?"

"What was it called again?"

"Chaldean. It's not as common as the Pythagorean System, but it's been around the longest, except for maybe Ki and Kabbalah, but those are based on different alphabets."

I couldn't help but laugh. "I thought you said you just dabbled."

"What can I say?" She smiled wryly. "It's a hobby."

"Isn't it kind of weird that there are so many systems?" I asked.

She toyed with her bracelets and they jangled softly. "Oh, I don't know. They're all attempts to understand the vibrations of the universe, I suppose."

"Vibrations?" I thought of the way my head buzzed whenever I was pulled into a trance. I would definitely describe that as vibration. "What does that mean?"

Gina blew her black hair from her eyes and looked up to the ceiling as if trying to divine the answer. "It's like . . . there's energy all around us, right? Lots of different kinds of energy, but it all occupies the same space. The thing that distinguishes the one from the other is a different wavelength."

"Okay," I said cautiously.

"Those wavelengths—the vibrations—are on what you might call different frequencies," she continued. "So it's possible to tune into, for instance, the energy vibrations of numbers if you hit the right frequency."

"Like a radio?" I asked.

"Exactly! Your brain is a receptor with electrical impulses running through it, right? So, theoretically, if you set your brain to the same vibratory wavelength as the energy you want to tune into, you draw that energy to you in the form of thoughts or impressions."

"By tuning into it."

She gave me a triumphant smile. "You've got it."

I almost couldn't believe it. Was she saying that I could actually control the vibrations? I was trying to figure out how to ask her when she suddenly pushed back from the table.

"Yikes. Break's over already." She pushed to her feet. "That was much too short. We're going to have to talk to Carole about that."

"Yeah," I murmured. I was vaguely aware of her leaving. I think I waved good-bye, but I'm not sure. I was too preoccupied considering the possibilities of what Gina had just said. If I had the power to control the vibrations, it might be possible to draw the trances to me. I might even be able to determine what it was I saw in them. If Kyra wouldn't help me to see whatever was in the vision, maybe I could do it myself.

If I could jump-start a trance, I'd have more control. I could choose when. I could choose where. Jumping up from the table, I tried to think of a secluded place in the mall where I could go to try it out. I glanced at my watch. I'd have to hurry—I had to be to work by five. There wasn't much time.

The great thing about the Nordstrom in the Westland Mall is that they have a lounge in the third-floor restroom. I assume it's meant for moms who want a discreet place to breast-feed their babies or something, because I can't imagine why else anyone would want to go hang out in a bathroom. Whatever the purpose, it was the perfect room to hide away and try my hand at "tuning in."

Just in case anyone walked in while I was experimenting, I turned one of the nursing chairs toward the wall before pulling out my notebook and pen. I sat and stared at the textured pattern of the wallpaper and, for the first time, challenged the trance to come to me.

I didn't have to wait long before a buzz started at the base of my skull and then exploded in my head. I heard my own gasp before I slipped away.

***

I'm back on the road. Numbers fill the space above my head. Colors running, dripping in the rain. I turn in a circle, watching in the darkness for the head-lights. There they are—distant pinpricks of light growing bigger with every heartbeat. And then I see him. The light's behind him, so all I can make out is a dark silhouette, but there's something familiar about him. I feel his panic as the headlights close in and I try to call to him, but he doesn't hear me. I can't see his face.

"Over here!" I yell, and he starts to turn.

With a strong *whoosh!* I was back in the lounge, the notebook paper covered in a string of numbers.

My mouth had gone completely dry and my heart was racing so fast it made my chest ache, but I had done it! I was in control. And then it hit me: if I could call on the trances, maybe I could learn to avoid them as well. Maybe I could make them stop. For the first time in months, I felt hope.

When I got back to ShutterBugz, Jake was leaning on the counter, talking to Gina. They must have been having some conversation, because neither one of them even noticed I had walked up beside them.

"What's going on?" I asked.

Gina about jumped off the stool. One hand flew to

her throat and the other to her stomach. "Don't *do* that! Do you want to see this baby drop out right at your feet?"

"Um, I don't think it works that way."

"Never mind." She grabbed her bag out from under the counter. "I didn't have this with me when we were talking in the food court. I brought something to show you." She started digging through the bag. I'd never seen her so animated.

I looked to Jake, questioning, but he just shrugged and gave me the universal "beats me" palms up.

She finally found what she was looking for—a carved wooden box. She held it up reverently, like we were supposed to be impressed.

"It's . . . really nice," I said.

She rolled her eyes. "Not the box, genius. I want to show you what's *in* the box." She dropped her bag to the floor and set the box on the counter. Both Jake and I leaned forward as she pulled off the top lid.

"I was thinking," she said, "about our conversation the other day and then I started wondering if I still had these and it turns out I did!"

I reached out to pick one up at the same time as Jake asked, "What are they?"

Gina smiled proudly. "My tarot cards."

I yanked my hand back like my fingers had been scorched and she laughed.

"They're not going to bite you or curse you, or whatever it is you're thinking."

"I'm not . . ." I started, but I couldn't put it into words. Everything I knew about tarot cards was associated with the occult. It had been drilled into me forever to be afraid of anything having to do with the occult. My trances included.

Gina tilted the box and let the cards fall out into her hand. "Remember how I was telling you how the Chaldean number vibrations have tarot associations? Well, I thought you might be interested in seeing what they are."

"Am I missing something?" Jake asked. "What is all this?"

Gina glanced at me quickly and then shrugged. "Just something Ashlyn and I were talking about." She pulled the top card from the deck and placed it faceup on the counter. It showed a man, hanging upside down from a tree. "Remember I told you about the victim number? This is the corresponding tarot image. And this"—she laid the next card down by the first—"is the Shattered Citadel." The card showed a man with a crown, falling headfirst from a tower that was being struck by lightning.

I remembered how Gina had said that number and symbol had something to do with strange fatalities. I shifted uncomfortably.

"But this one," she said, laying down the next card, "is one of my favorites. It's 'The Awakening.' Here's the angel with the trumpet." She pointed to the illustration at the top of the card. "But this is the only deck I have with the little angel girls rising to meet him."

Suddenly, the light around me narrowed until it felt like I was looking through a long, dark tunnel. The only image I could see was the illustration on the card—two little angels, dressed in white. My throat closed and my breath became shallow and tight. I wanted to look away, but my eyes were pulled toward it.

"That's cool," Jake said, "But what's it for?"

The pull was broken. I blinked and the light returned. Gina was gathering her cards, tapping the deck on the counter to straighten them.

"Some people," she said matter-of-factly, "believe you can use the cards, or numbers, or other metaphysical signals to predict the future."

"Do *you* believe in it?" I asked.

Jake laughed. "She believes in everything."

She shot him a look and laid the cards gently back in their case. "Hey, watch your tone. You're talking about someone's mom here. And I don't believe in *everything*, thank you. I don't believe in bigotry. I don't believe in small-mindedness, I don't believe—"

Laughing, he threw up his hands in surrender. "You win, as always."

Gina dipped her head regally. "Thank you for acknowledging it."

"I know when I've been beat." He backed away from the kiosk. "I better get to work."

Gina waved him off and then turned to me, her eyes alight. "You're going to love this. Just for giggles, while you were off shopping, I decided to do all our numbers. What do you think?"

"Yeah, that would be fun," I said cautiously.

She grinned and pulled out a paper from her purse. "It *was* fun. So check out what I found for you." She pointed to the paper. "I didn't have your birth date, so I just ran your number vibrations based on your name."

On the paper, my name was written across the top, with the corresponding numbers below. She added the numbers in a string that looked exactly like the way Kyra and I wrote when we were in a trance.

A S H L Y N   G R E E N F I E L D
1+3+5+3+1+5 = 18   3+2+5+5+5+8+1+5+3+4 = 41
1+8 = 9   4+1 = 5

9+5 = 14
1+4 = 5

"Your compound vibration numbers are these," she said, and circled the numbers eighteen, forty-one, and fourteen. "What I get from them is that you are powerful and mysterious. Eighteen is a tough one to read because it can point to so many things. It talks about the world trying to destroy the spiritual power. We'll leave that one alone for a minute. 'Cause we've got this bad boy right here." She pointed to the number forty-one. "This number is supposed to have magical power and deals with future events and so does this one." She pointed to the fourteen. "This also talks about danger from natural forces like water, fire, air, that sort of thing."

I stared at the paper. The equations looked the same as what I was used to, but something was off. "I don't understand," I said. "How are you getting these numbers?"

Gina glanced up, frowning. "What do you mean?"

"I've had my numbers done before and these aren't them."

She thought for a moment and then the understanding lit her face. "Oh, right. I see where you're confused. Remember how I told you about the Chaldeans?"

Not really, but I nodded hesitantly anyway. "Yeah?"

"The number values they assigned to each letter were different than what the Pythagoreans did." She flipped the paper over and grabbed a pen. "The Chaldeans didn't assign any letters to the number nine because nine is considered sacred. That's why their number-to-letter calculations are different than what you get with the Pythagorean System. Look, I'll show you." She listed the numbers one through nine across the top of one half of the paper, and the numbers one through eight on the other. "Now watch," she said, and began scribbling letters in columns beneath the numbers.

1	2	3	4	5	6	7	8	9
A	B	C	D	E	F	G	H	I
J	K	L	M	N	O	P	Q	R
S	T	U	V	W	X	Y	Z	

1	2	3	4	5	6	7	8
A	B	C	D	E	U	O	F
I	K	G	M	H	V	Z	P
J	R	L	T	N	W		
Q		S		X			
Y							

"See? This is how the numbers come out differently."

"I see." I stared at the different number associations and shook my head. It made sense in a tragic kind of way. All those years, Kyra and I had been trying to decipher the messages we wrote by using the Pythagorean values for number vibrations. We never even considered another system.

Gina didn't seem to sense my change of mood but rattled on, grinning like we were sharing some cosmic joke. "Now, what's cool," she said, flipping the paper back over, "is when we reduce the numbers. So with your first name, we take the one and eight and you have nine. You see, the sacred number. And the four and one from your last name gives us five, which is supposed to be a perfect number. It means 'stops the power of poisons.' Both of those numbers have very powerful vibrations. So you, my dear, are a magical, powerful soothsayer with the ability to stop poisons!"

She laughed and I tried to laugh with her. It was stupid, really. I wasn't even sure I believed in numerology, so I shouldn't have been so shaken. But the two angels on the tarot card, the different numbering systems, the mention of the future from the compound numbers in Gina's reading . . . it all hit too close to home.

Gina handed me the paper. "Here. You keep it." She was about to sling the strap of her bag up over her shoulder when she stopped. "Oh, do you want to know something really fun? You and Jake have the exact same first name, last name, and final number vibrations. How wild is that?" She elbowed me in the side.

I was so thrown by the Chaldean connection that I didn't recognize the tease. "What does that mean?" I asked, completely serious.

Gina threw back her head and laughed. "I tell you what," she said. "I'm going to let you figure that out."

It took a little time for the information Gina had given me to sink in. After the initial pang of realizing how Kyra and I could have missed the mark for all those years, the thought occurred to me that understanding the new numbers could change everything. We had never been able to make sense of the messages we wrote, but maybe now we could. It wouldn't be easy—we'd still be working the numbers to letters backward with a huge range of possibilities, but at least we might come closer than we had before. Pair that with my success in the Nordstrom lounge and I wasn't helpless anymore.

My mood took such an upswing that the ShutterBugz kiosk was much too small to contain my new infusion of energy and enthusiasm. I wanted to run, to shout, to hug everyone I met. I knew I was being too smiley, too bouncy.

People probably thought I was insane, but I didn't care. If I could control the trances, there was nothing I couldn't do.

I couldn't wait to tell Kyra, to teach her how to "tune in." She may not want to talk to me now, but she would change her mind once she knew what I had to say. Then she could come home. Then we could learn the power of the vibrations together.

I pulled out the numbers Gina had done for me and ran my fingers over the compound numbers she had circled. She said they meant I was powerful. I *felt* powerful.

And Jake. I peeked up at the Kinnear Music window, smiling at the idea that he and I had the same numbers. I added them in my head. J, A, K, E, 1, 1, 2, 5. He didn't have a compound vibration, but the total added up to nine, just like mine. But then I started to do the last name and paused. Gina said the numbers were exactly the same, but Kinnear's compound number added up to twenty-one, which would be reduced to three. Greenfield was forty-one, which is how I got the perfect number of five.

She must have made a mistake. Or maybe I did, adding in my head. I was about to take out a pen and write it down when the phone rang. It was Carole, reminding me to prepare the deposit for the night, like this was a new task for me. I was in such a good mood, I didn't even let it bother me.

I had just started dragging the gate around the kiosk that

night when I noticed Nick sitting at a table in the food court, watching me. I'd made such a habit of feeling small around Nick that I almost lost some of my newly gained confidence, seeing him there. But then I remembered: there was nothing I couldn't do.

I waved to him and he raised his chin to me in that I'm-so-cool way. I smiled to myself and continued locking up. When I turned around, he was standing right behind me.

"Oh!" I gasped. "You startled me."

He took a step back, that cool aura gone. "I'm sorry."

"That's okay. I was just—"

"No," he said. He dug his hands into his pockets and stared at his feet. "I mean, I really am sorry. I just wanted you to know."

He turned to walk away, but I grabbed his arm. "Wait."

Nick looked back toward me, but he wouldn't look *at* me. "I don't blame you for hating me," he said.

A hot knot tightened in my throat. Is that what he thought? "I don't hate you, Nick," I said softly.

He stared at his feet some more.

"Come on." I led him to an empty bench near the center court. "Let's talk."

It's interesting what a change in perspective can do. For the first time, I found myself looking at Nick not as a boy I'd had a crush on for four years, but as a person who was hurting inside, just like I was. I realized, as I looked at him with all the swagger stripped away, that the only power he'd ever held over me was the power I had given him.

I took his hand.

He finally raised his eyes to mine. "I saw you," he said, "at the mall. And when I heard about the accident . . ."

"Nick . . ."

"If I'd have known what would happen . . ."

I swallowed. How many times had I said that to myself? "It wasn't your fault."

He nodded and I wasn't sure if he was agreeing or disagreeing with me. "I'm sorry about your mom."

I squeezed his hand. "Thank you."

We walked out to the mall parking lot, talking about nothing in particular. I could almost see the weight of the guilt Nick had been carrying around slowly ease off his shoulders. I could absolutely feel the feelings of inadequacy slough off mine. By the time we said good-bye, I was beginning to feel like I could move mountains.

I had never known such a feeling of control. I could do anything! I was magical, powerful.

I turned toward home and had just crossed the street when I heard Jake's bike rumbling up behind me. He pulled up to the curb and stopped, engine idling.

"You're walking?" he shouted over the noise.

"Missed the bus," I yelled.

"Where's your friend?"

I stepped closer so I could hear him. "Michelle? Hot study date."

He shook his head. "No. Your *other* friend."

I realized he must have seen Nick and me together. "He's gone."

"Lovers' spat?"

I looked to see if he was joking, but his face looked completely serious. "That's not . . . he's not . . ."

He couldn't hold back the smile any longer. "Come on, I'll give you a ride. If you want."

I did want. I wanted in a big way. And for once, now that I felt like I was in control, I thought I wouldn't have to worry. "Thanks."

He handed me a helmet and I put it on—correctly this time. I climbed onto the seat behind him and took a deep breath, leaning in close, wrapping my arms around him. This time it felt comfortable. This time it felt right.

We didn't make it far. By the time we reached the tree-lined streets off the main drag, his Indian started sputtering. A block later it backfired, then growled, then died. He steered the bike to the side of the road and we rolled to a stop.

"I don't believe it," he muttered.

"What's wrong?"

"I have no idea. I'd have to look at it in the light."

We climbed off the motorcycle and for a moment Jake just stood there with his arms folded across his chest, staring down the Indian like it had betrayed him.

"I'm sorry," I offered.

He turned to me. "What? No, *I'm* sorry. And embarrassed."

I laughed. "You don't have to be embarrassed around me."

"But I am just the same." He locked the helmets into the seat compartment. "Come on. I'll walk you home."

"You don't have to do that," I said. "It's not that far."

"I don't have to do a lot of things." He bowed low and swept his arm in the direction we should walk. "Shall we?"

"What about your motorcycle?"

"I'll come back and get it. No big deal."

"What are you going to do, roll it home?"

"If I have to." He took my elbow and dragged me along for a few steps before he let go. "I've walked it home from a lot farther than this."

"Really. Where do you live?"

"Not too far. Over on Hague."

I stopped walking. "Hague? That's clear on the other side of town."

He shrugged and pulled me forward again. "Gina did that number thing for me, you know. She said I was powerful, so I just think I should warn you. It's futile to resist."

I laughed at that, but wondered if Gina had also told him that our numbers were the same.

"Now you know something about me," he said. "Tell me something I don't know about you."

It shouldn't have been so hard to think of something, but I never talked about myself; I had too many secrets. I couldn't think of anything about me that I could talk about. "Can I make up something?"

"Nothing but the truth," he said, and held up three fingers in a kind of salute.

"What's that?" I giggled. "The Spock Pledge?"

He shook his head sadly. "You lose serious geek points for that. No, it was not the Vulcan salute. It was the Boy Scout sign."

I laughed even more. "You were a Boy Scout?"

"Nice try. You already got one on me. You have to tell me something about yourself now. Truthfully."

I kicked at the gravel on the street and tried to think of something real that would keep things light. It was too hard. "I have one sister and no pets" was all I could come up with.

"Weak," he said. "But I'll accept it. And yes, I was in the Boy Scouts, but that was a long time ago. Your turn."

"Uh, who decided we were going to play this game?"

He bumped my arm with his. "You seem to be forgetting I'm powerful. No questions."

"Okay." I took a deep breath. "I can't smell skunk. I'm not a smeller. We did one of those PTC paper tests in science once and I'm not a taster, either."

"I don't think," he said, "that you're serious about engaging in this conversation."

I laughed. "And I think your power has gone to your head."

"Mysterious and stubborn. I like it."

"You're kidding me. Gina told you I was mysterious?"

He gave me a weird look. "Gina?"

"Yeah, the numerology thing. She said I was mysterious. . . ." My voice trailed off and I felt really stupid.

Jake laughed. "So I was right, only I was talking about your evasive answers."

I was glad it was dark so he couldn't tell how red my face was getting. "Oh."

"Sorry to tell you," he said, "but powerful trumps mysterious."

"No problem. I happen to be powerful *and* mysterious."

We stepped out from under the tree branches and Jake immediately looked up. "Look," he said, and pointed to the sky.

For the first time in weeks, the sky was completely clear. We had a perfect view of the stars. Jake put one hand on my shoulder and turned me slightly toward him. I held my breath in anticipation.

"See that one over there?" He pointed skyward again. "Three stars in a row? That's Orion's belt."

I looked up at him and grinned. "Boy Scouts?"

He shrugged. "It's the only constellation I learned. I was trying to impress you."

"Aw, that's—"

When I felt the tremor, I wasn't sure what it was. I froze for an instant until I could feel it centering at the back of my head, humming, buzzing. The corners of my vision dimmed like a fading photograph. I drew in a quick breath. Not again.

All the control and confidence and invincibility I'd been feeling disappeared in an instant. I was still me. Small. Helpless. Powerless against the trances.

I backed away from Jake. I shouldn't have come with him. I couldn't let him see.

"Everything okay?" he said.

Not even close. It didn't make any sense. The visions always came with the writing and I wasn't carrying anything to write *with*. Maybe that's why my head was buzzing like a chain saw, but I wasn't getting sucked in. Yet. Or maybe I had changed the rules when I called on the latest trance. Whatever the case, I had to get away. Right now.

"I can run home from here," I said. "But thanks for the escort."

He had a confused look on his face, like someone had snuck up and smacked him on the back of the head. "But—"

"It's just . . . You've got a long way to push that bike and—"

"Did I miss something?"

"No. No. I . . . I'll see you around." I spun around and ran before he could say anything more.

By the time I got home, my heart was banging in my chest like it was trapped and wanted out. I let myself into the house and immediately felt the painful squeeze when I looked at my mom's parlor. I stumbled down the hallway, grateful for once that I was alone.

In the kitchen, I turned my face to the ceiling. "What do you want from me?" I cried.

Upending my backpack on the kitchen table, I grabbed my notebook and pencil once more. "You want me to write? I'll write! Just tell me what I'm supposed to *do!*"

The next morning I woke to the chime of the clock in the hallway. One, two, three . . . I had fallen asleep, slumped in a chair at the kitchen table. Four, five . . . The vibration in my head had never resulted in a trance, no matter how I had yelled and pleaded and tried to force it to come. So much for control. Six.

I bolted up, suddenly wide awake. Six o'clock! Michelle would be here any minute. I jumped to my feet, adrenaline pumping, before I remembered that she wouldn't be running with me that morning. She was on her way to the track meet—the meet I should have been going to.

I slogged back to my room and crawled into my bed. I may as well get used to staying home, I grumbled. I didn't know how I was going to get a doctor's note to get back in the game. Would they request any kind of blood or urine tests for a health clearance? Would the pills I had taken the other day show up? If so, my season would be over, and possibly my career.

The whole thing was so depressing, I pulled the covers over my head and went back to sleep.

The sun was shining brightly through my window when my ringing cell phone woke me again. I dragged my backpack into the bed with me and fumbled around inside until I found the phone. I checked the screen to see who it was and, for an instant, I was disoriented again. Carole. Wait. Was I late for work? But no, I wasn't scheduled; I was *supposed* to be at the track meet. "Hello?"

"Oh, Ashlyn! Thank heavens you answered! Danae called in sick just five minutes ago and here we are two weeks before Easter and the mall will be packed and I need someone to fill in for her." She paused for a breath. "Can you come in? Could you take the afternoon shift, say, one to eight?"

I toyed with the strap of my backpack. I really wasn't in the mood to deal with the craziness of ShutterBugz. But I didn't want to be alone, either. And I did need the money. The afternoon shift probably wouldn't be too bad; most of the rush was typically in the morning. Besides, now that I wasn't going to be at the meet, I'd have nothing to do all day. Dad was still gone and the house would be sad and empty. "Sure," I said. "I can be there."

"Oh, thank you!" she gushed. "You're the best!" She gave me a long list of instructions—as if I had never worked a Saturday before—and rang off.

I flopped back against my pillow and stared at the ceiling. Before I even wondered who I would be paired with for the day, my mind went to Jake. Would he be working, too? I hoped he would, but then I hoped he wouldn't. How was I going to face him? How would I explain why I kept running away?

I took my running gear with me to work. Since I had been lazy and hadn't run that morning, and since Michelle and I never ran on Sundays, I figured I should at least get the exercise of running home from the mall. On top of everything else, I didn't want to feel like a slug.

When I got to the mall, I listened for the piano music, but all I could hear was the canned stuff they played over the intercom. I hoped maybe I'd catch a glimpse of Jake at the baby grand, but the piano bench in the window of Kinnear Music was empty.

Carole waved to me when she saw me coming. "Oh, there you are! Gina thought you might be late, but I said to her, I said, 'Ashlyn was always on time at Polaris,' and here you are!"

Her hot pink mouth curved into a self-satisfied smile.

Carole told me once how her sister had insisted that the pink colors Carole loved so much clashed with her red hair. *So I wear pink all the time, just to bug her*, she said. If she wasn't wearing pink shoes, she was wearing a pink scarf, a pink jacket, or a pink shirt. One time, much to everyone's dismay, she even wore pink jeans to the ShutterBugz kiosk at Polaris.

Gina poked her head out from behind the partition. "Finally!" she said. "I'm about to explode."

I dropped my backpack behind the counter. "I'm five minutes early," I told her, but she didn't answer. She just rushed off toward the food court.

Carole clucked, watching her go. "I do hope that baby comes soon. There's no living with her some days." She glanced back at me over her shoulder. "I'm glad *you* get along with her at least. She's a little too intense for some people."

I shrugged and slipped on my apron. "She's just . . . Gina."

Carole chuckled. "Well said."

I flushed, remembering how Jake had said it first. My gaze immediately snapped to Kinnear Music, but I still saw no sign of him. It was probably just as well. As much as I wanted to explain the night before, what was I supposed to *say*? It would be best for both of us if I just left him alone.

" . . . and then after I go it'll be just you and Gina for

the rest of the day, okay?" Carole was looking at me expectantly, waiting for an answer, I realized.

"Uh, sure," I said, hoping I hadn't just agreed to work for free or something like that.

That seemed to satisfy Carole. She straightened the pencil can and then continued her monologue, tugging on one of her short red curls. "I hate to schedule her for so many hours, but she needs the money, poor thing. Such a difficult situation."

I finished tying my apron strings and glanced up. "Situation?" The question slipped out before I could stop myself. I admit to being curious, but I also figured that whatever Gina's story was, it was hers to tell me. I'd already opened the door, though, and Carole danced right through it.

She lowered her voice conspiratorially. "Her husband's family. Nasty people. She's staying with them while her husband's deployed." She made a sour face. "They think she's not good enough for them because her people don't have money. And . . . well, you know, she *had* to get married. But the way they treat her! As if she was one of those girls who 'traps' rich boys by getting themselves pregnant. Now I ask you, how does a girl get *herself* pregnant?"

She paused as if she really wanted me to answer that question.

"Well, I told her," she continued, "I said, 'Gina, you can come live with me until Danny gets home.' That's her husband, Daniel, but I call him Danny, of course."

"Of course," I murmured. I knew I should stop her, that I only encouraged her by listening.

"But Gina, she says she needs to try and get along with them. For Danny. Did you know he won't be here when the baby comes? Can't get leave. And those people—" She shook her head, curls quivering. "I can't imagine what good they'll be to her. But you never hear her talk about them. Honestly, Ashlyn, she's so outspoken about everything else, I don't know how she keeps it all inside, I just don't. Now, come take a look at the new tracking system."

By the time Gina returned from lunch, Carole had reviewed with me, three times, how to track the digital portrait files—not exactly new since I'd been doing it since my days at Polaris.

The moment Gina slid her purse back under the counter, Carole was in motion, straightening the pencils, rearranging the order forms on the clipboard, picking up her things. "All right, then, Ashlyn is all set to help you out, hon. You let me know if you need me to come back in."

Gina took Carole by her pink shoulders and turned her around. "Get out of here, already. Go."

"What did I tell you?" Carole said, chuckling. "No living with her." And with that, she was finally gone.

"Whew." Gina backed to the stool and sat down. "That woman is exhausting! Good heart, but exhausting."

I murmured my agreement.

"So what did you two talk about while I was gone?"

My face suddenly felt cold. "Oh. Nothing. I mean . . ."

She pushed her curtain of dark hair over her shoulder. "It's okay. I know Carole. She can't keep her mouth shut sometimes. So, what'd she tell you? About my awful in-laws?"

I just shrugged, trying not to think about all the things Carole had said.

"They're not so bad." Gina's hands went to her belly and she rubbed it absently. "Nope. I lied. They suck."

"Why do you live with them, then?" I blurted.

She snorted a laugh. "Oh, so you *were* talking about me. My family is . . . kind of a mess, so when Daniel deployed, he thought I should live with his family while he was gone so they could 'take care of me.'"

"But if you don't like them—"

"I never said that." Her face grew serious. "Do I like living with Daniel's family? No. Would I ever tell him that? No. I know I'm all about honesty and saying what I think, but sometimes people are more important than the truth."

15

We probably did about five or six sittings that afternoon, but only one stuck out in my mind—two little girls who could have passed for twins, they looked so much alike.

"No, just sisters," the mother assured me. *Just sisters.*

They were probably the best-behaved kids we'd had in there all week. Both girls sat still, kept their hands where I placed them, and looked up innocently where I told them to look. But the mother kept calling out directions anyway.

"Sit up straight, Olivia! Straight, like we practiced. No. Not like that. Abby, what did we say about smiling? Shoulders back. Chin up."

It made me sad to watch, because both of those little girls were perfect, but their mom couldn't see it. She must have had some picture in her mind of what the perfect portrait should look like, and it didn't matter how well her daughters cooperated or how many other great shots we got, she wasn't satisfied because it wasn't what she had in mind. But the saddest part was watching the faces of the girls as they tried desperately to please their mother, only to fall short again and again.

I knew what that was like.

"Hope your car windows are rolled up," Gina said as she got back from her break. "It looks like it's going to storm out there."

Oh, great, I thought. *There goes my run.* "How bad does it look?"

"Nothing starting yet, but I wouldn't be surprised if we drive home in a downpour."

I looked anxiously beyond the food court. From where we were situated, I couldn't see to the doors that led outside, but I hoped I might be able to tell how bright it was out there.

"What's wrong?" Gina asked.

"I was planning on running home," I told her.

"Yikes." She looked up from the receipts. "How far do you live?"

I shrugged. "Two miles, maybe. Three, tops."

Her mouth hung open. "You're going to *run* that? Are you insane?"

"I run the 5K in cross country. It's about the same distance."

"Too much work for me." She went back to tallying the totals.

I looked toward the food court again. "Would you mind if I changed real quick? If it's going to start raining, I want to take off as soon I can."

She glanced up and tucked her hair behind her ear. "You can just go. I'm almost done here."

"Are you sure?"

She glowered at me. "You want me to change my mind?"

I gave her a quick hug. "Thanks, Gina. You're the best!"

She pulled back, looking stunned. "Go on. Get out of here."

I grabbed my backpack and sprinted to the women's restroom to change out of my work clothes. By the time I made it outside, the clouds hung low and dark. The air felt heavy but it didn't *smell* like rain yet. I was willing to take my chances. Since I didn't have much time, I abbreviated the stretching and warm-ups and then took off.

About halfway across the parking lot, I thought I heard a voice behind me, calling my name. I glanced over my shoulder and my breath caught. Jake was running to catch up with me. He *was* at work! I wondered why I hadn't seen him all day.

I jogged in place as I waited. "What's going on?"

"You left early," he said. "I wanted to talk to you."

"Yeah? What's up?"

He slowed to a walk as he approached me. "You doing anything tonight?"

"Running," I said.

He grinned. "After that."

"Why?"

"You want to go out or something?"

Go out? How fair was that? I would have loved to go out with him, more than anything in the world, but not when I could slip into a trance at any moment. "I can't."

His face fell, and I felt awful. More than awful. I was miserable. I turned around and started running again.

He followed. "Is there something wrong?"

Yes. Everything. But I shook my head, no.

"Did I *do* something? 'Cause it seems like you're always running away from me. Should I be getting a complex here?"

My heart tumbled. *No, it isn't you.* "I . . . I just can't get involved with anyone right now."

"I'm not talking about getting 'involved,'" he said. "I'm talking about dinner."

"I'm sorry."

He kept up with me, stride for stride, even though I knew his motorcycle boots weren't made for running. "You do eat, right?"

"Look, no offense, but I'm in training."

"Got it. We'll only eat healthy food."

I gritted my teeth. He was making it hard. "No, I mean right now. I need to run. I have a meet in a couple of weeks."

"Time or distance?"

"What?"

He gave me another cockeyed smile. "Are you going for time or distance?"

I was perversely pleased to note that he was beginning to sound out of breath. "Both," I said. "I run the 3200 so I'm working on endurance *and* time."

"So we should go faster, right?" He sped up just enough to pull ahead of me.

I dug in so that our strides were matched again. "*We* shouldn't do anything," I puffed. "I run alone."

"I can take a hint," he said. "I'll be quiet." He kept the pace beside me, his footsteps stomp, stomp, stomping the pavement in perfect rhythm with mine.

By then, I figured that arguing with him wasn't getting me anywhere, so I decided to ignore him instead. Of course, that would have been a lot easier if he didn't keep inching into the lead. It was hard to lose myself in the run when I kept seeing him out of the corner of my eye, pulling ahead of me. There was no way I was going to let some musician in clunky motorcycle boots show me up. By the time we reached the fire hydrant at the end of my block where I always ended my run, my lungs were burning and my mouth felt like it had been dragged through the Kalahari.

I burst through my imaginary finish line and slowed to a jog, then a fast walk, sucking in air.

Jake walked in circles nearby, hands clasped behind his head as he tried to catch his breath. He gestured at my wristwatch with his head. "How'd we do?"

I realized that I had completely forgotten about the time. "Fine."

"So," he said. "Are you hungry?"

"Look, Jake. I would love to go out with you but—"

"No, no. You've got it all wrong. The correct answer is 'yes.'"

He looked so vulnerable standing there with his shirt soaked in sweat, his stupid music-note tie askew, his hair all tousled from the wind . . . and yet, he was still grinning. I wished I could have that kind of confidence.

"Look, Jake—"

That was when it began to rain. Not just a gentle shower, but an icy torrent, sudden and angry. We were both soaked through in seconds.

"Come on!" I yelled, and motioned for him to follow me. We ran down the street to my house, splashing along the sidewalk with every step.

At the front door, we ducked under the roof overhang as I fished my keys out of my sodden backpack. I unlocked the door and we stepped inside the house, shivering and dripping. It felt strange, coming home and not being alone. Strange in a good way.

Inside the hallway, I flipped on the lights and as much as I tried to resist it, my eyes were drawn immediately to my mom's couch. I was afraid I might see her sitting there, shaking her head in disapproval. It was empty as always.

"Nice place," Jake said.

"Thanks." I stuffed my keys into my backpack. "My mom loved to decorate." I wondered if he caught the catch in my throat at the word *mom*.

I dropped my backpack to the floor and kicked off my shoes. "Stay here," I said. "I'll get you something to dry off with."

When I ducked into my bathroom to grab the towels, I caught a glimpse of myself in the mirror. My hair was a mess—tangled and stringy wet—my makeup was gone and my clothes were smeared with mud, but for the first time in months, the eyes that looked back at me were bright, eager. A flush of color warmed my cheeks. I quickly ran a comb through my hair to smooth it down and hurried back to where Jake waited, dripping, in the hallway.

"Here you go." I handed him one of the towels, and spread the others on the floor to wipe up the water we had tracked in. He bent to help me and our hands touched. His eyes met mine and suddenly, I felt shy. I gathered the towels and stood quickly.

"If, um . . . if you want to come on back to the laundry

room, I can give you something to put on and we can stick your clothes in the dryer. If you want."

He gave me a reassuring smile. "That's okay." He held up his towel. "I'm good."

"Well, I need to get out of my running clothes. Make yourself at home. I'll be right back."

In my room, I slipped quickly into my old, comfy jeans and my Springfield hoodie. I pulled my hair back into a quick ponytail, trying not to think about what I was doing. Thinking made me question and I didn't want any more questions.

Outside, the storm blew and howled. Rain beat on the roof, thunder rattled the windows. But inside, it was safe and warm and normal, and that was enough to know. For just one night, I wanted to be a regular girl spending time with the boy she liked. That didn't seem too much to ask.

16

Jake had kicked off his boots and peeled off his dress shirt and tie. He stood in the front hall in his jeans and white T-shirt—just like on the first night I saw him. A flush of pleasure followed the memory of him on his Indian. I smiled until I saw that he was examining the pictures on the living wall. I walked quickly toward him. *Don't ask. Don't ask. Don't . . .*

But he passed up the photos of my mom and pointed to one of me in a purple tutu with fairy wings from my third-grade Halloween party. "Niiice," he said. "Good look for you."

"Thanks. I'll remember that." I flipped off the light in the hall and led him back to the kitchen. "Do you want something to drink? We have Gatorade, milk, orange juice . . ."

"Water?"

"You got it." I grabbed two glasses from the cupboard and filled them with ice. My hands were shaking more than they should, but I chalked it up to nerves. I poured the water from a pitcher in the fridge and handed his glass to him, and we stood in awkward silence as we both drank.

"It's so quiet in here," Jake said finally. "Where is everybody?"

"My dad's out of town on business," I said, and set the glass on the counter. I brushed past him to the great room before he could ask for any details. "You want to watch a movie or something until this storm dies down? My dad's a Bond fanatic if you like action. We have every Bond movie ever made, although, to me, there is only one, true Bond."

He followed me into the great room and flopped down onto the couch. "Who? Roger Moore?"

"Ew. No. Sean Connery all the way. No one can even *say* James Bond the way Sean Connery can."

"What about Daniel Craig?"

I dug through the DVD drawers. "Nope. Nice to look at, but his movies were straight action. Not classic Bond."

"A Bond connoisseur. I'm impressed."

"Yeah, well." I sifted through the Sean Connery titles, selecting *Dr. No*, *Goldfinger*, and *You Only Live Twice*. "It gave me something to do with my dad." I dropped the DVDs on the ottoman and headed into the kitchen. "Okay, those are the classics of the classics. You choose which one and I'll make the popcorn."

When I walked back into the room, the DVDs were still on the ottoman and Jake was looking at something else. He glanced up at me.

"What's this?" In his hands was my journal.

I stopped cold. I had forgotten it was still there. "Nothing," I said too quickly.

His brows shot up. "Really."

"Yeah." I dropped onto the couch and set the popcorn bowl on the ottoman. "Just a bunch of pictures."

He turned the page. "A bunch of really good pictures. Did you take these?"

I tried to wrench the book out of his hands. "Let's watch the movie."

He held on tight. "You're avoiding."

"I am not," I said automatically.

"Denial," he said.

I let go of the book and turned away from him in a huff. "Are we going to watch the movie or not?"

"Soon." He stretched his legs out in front of him and crossed one foot over the other. "Tell me about these. I'm interested."

I couldn't make myself speak for several seconds. But there was no judgment in Jake's eyes. Nothing but sincerity. "It's my journal," I said finally.

He looked down at the pages again. "A photo journal. Nice."

I raised my shoulders. "I guess."

"What is this?" he asked. He pointed to the photo on the first page.

I scooted closer to him so I could see. "That's the pattern left in the sand from the waves where we were on a family vacation in South Carolina. See how it looks like stalks and leaves? And this one"—I turned the page—"is the same beach with little craters left in the sand after it rained."

"Oh, yeah," he said.

I ran my fingers over the picture. "We were stuck inside for three days on that trip because it kept pouring. My parents had rented a cabin out in the boonies, so there was nothing to do but hang out together." I remembered how Kyra and I had found a pack of Uno cards in one of the kitchen drawers and made up about ten different card games during those long days. We even got Mom and Dad to play with us a couple of times and it was like they were kids like us, the way they argued over the rules. "It's one of my favorite memories."

"Interesting." He flipped through several more pages. "And this?"

"That's from when I went on a walk with my dad in the fall a couple of years ago. These are some leaves that were caught in the crevice of a rock. I liked how they looked protected there. Safe."

"I didn't see any pictures of people in here. Do you ever take pictures of people?"

"No," I said flatly.

"Except for the portraits at the mall."

"Except for those."

He closed the book. "You're just a walking contradiction, aren't you?"

I reached up to scratch the back of my neck. "I suppose."

It took a few seconds to realize what was happening. Why my neck was itching. My stomach lurched and I dropped my hand. Already, I could feel the darkness closing in. I shook my head, trying to fight the panic tumbling through my chest.

If I could start a trance, I could stall it. Right? I tried to tune out of the vibration. To think about something else. Anything to keep the trance from taking over.

"Are you okay?" Jake asked.

"Yeah. I just . . . I forgot something." I stood unsteadily, but managed to keep my balance. "I'll be right back."

My whole skull was vibrating by the time I reached my room. I swiped at a tear with the back of my hand. Just one night. Why couldn't I have just one night?

I staggered over to my desk and dropped into the chair. Picked up a pencil. *Okay*, I thought. *Let's have it.*

Immediately, my room disappeared.

***

*I'm standing on the same dark road. Shivering. Wet. I
blink away the rain and look toward the road. He is
standing where I saw him last. Still. Watching. I try to
call to him, but my voice makes no sound.* I can help,
*I cry silently. Just show me your face. But, of course,
he can't hear.*

> *I run to him, but the road gets wider with every
> step. Before I can reach him, a car speeds past. It
> spins me around. I can feel myself falling. . . .*

I jerked out of the trance as if I had physically been thrown
back. To keep from falling off the chair, I grabbed for the
desk, but my flailing hands only succeeded in knocking
my lamp and the flowerpot onto the floor. I tumbled down
after them.

When it hit the ground, the flowerpot shattered, scat-
tering coins and folded paper like confetti. My hand landed
right on top of one of the broken pieces of terra-cotta and
pain sliced through my palm. I cried out before I could
stop myself.

Blood welled up from the cut and I hugged my hand
close. And then I heard footsteps. Too soon, Jake stood in
the doorway.

"You all right?" he asked.

I sat up straight. "Yes. Uh. I'm fine, I just . . . I knocked
this over. I'll be right out."

He took a step inside the room. "You want me to help?"

I took one look at all the folded notes lying among the ceramic and drew in a sharp breath. "No! I mean . . . that's okay. I'm just about done."

He looked unsure, but he turned away. I could hear him walking back out to the family room, settling onto the couch. Quickly, I gathered the papers and the broken pieces and dumped them into the desk drawer to deal with later. As I pushed to my feet, I saw the latest note on the desk, so I grabbed it and stuffed it into the drawer with the rest of the papers. I didn't even have to look at it to know what numbers were written on it. I practically had this sequence memorized by now.

In the bathroom, I ran my hand under the faucet. Blood and water swirled pink down the drain. Grabbing a towel, I pressed it against the cut until it stopped bleeding. It didn't take long, but there was a noticeable red slice in the skin. I tried to cover it with a bandage, but I couldn't grasp the edges of the adhesive well enough to peel back the paper, so I gave up.

When I walked back out to join him on the couch, Jake was sitting stiffly on the edge, hands dangling between his knees. He looked up as I entered the room and gave me a wary look. "You okay?" he asked cautiously.

"I'm fine." I sank down onto the couch next to him. "Cut my hand, though." I held it out for him to examine. Better to head off any questions before they arose.

He visibly relaxed, leaning back against the cushions, and gently lifted my hand. "Does it hurt?"

"Not bad." I rested my head on the cushions next to his.

"Doesn't look too deep," he said. "I've had worse."

"Oh, we're comparing scars now, are we?"

"This is hardly a scar."

"What about this?" I reached up and traced the line above his cheek with my fingers. He flinched and I pulled my hand away, afraid I'd been too bold, but he caught it in his.

"Sliding glass door," he said. "Wrestling on the deck with my brother."

"Ouch."

"It was a long time ago."

"Ah."

"So, you like photography." He turned to look at me so that our foreheads were almost touching. So close that my breath caught and I had to force myself to breathe normally.

"Yeah. I really do," I said softly. I hadn't realized until I said it that it was true. I missed the way I saw the world when I was looking through the viewfinder. "What about you. Piano?"

"Music in general. Current love is bass guitar."

I thought back to what Gina had said. "Oh, yeah. Two-thousand-dollar amps."

"Yeah, well . . ." He wove his fingers through mine. "Someday."

"Do you get an employee discount at Kinnear?"

He laughed. "Uncle Dale doesn't carry amps. And if he did, he wouldn't give *me* a discount on them."

"Oh. Not a favorite uncle, I take it."

"Not so much."

The conversation died, but I was content just to sit there on the couch with him. "Which movie did you want to watch?" I asked finally.

"*Goldfinger?*"

"Is that a question?"

"Either that one or *Dr. No.*"

"How about both?" I held my breath, watching from under my eyelashes. Was that too long to expect him to hang out with me?

He thought about it for maybe half a second and then picked up *Dr. No.* "Let's start with the original."

I ducked my head to hide my smile and took the DVD from him to slip into the player. He wanted to stay! Even after all the weirdness, he wanted to stay with me.

When I returned to sit down, Jake had stretched his arm out across the back of the couch. I dropped back down beside him close enough that when he let his arm slip from the couch cushions to my shoulders, it was the perfect fit.

We finished *Dr. No* and started in with *Goldfinger.* By

the time Bond was escaping the Auric Industries plant in his custom Aston Martin, the popcorn was long gone and Jake's arm rested snug around my shoulders. I glanced up at him to comment on the car at the same time as he turned to me to say the same thing and we laughed.

Then Jake's laughter faded. He looked at me for a moment, suddenly serious as his fingers traced the side of my jaw. He lifted my chin and his lips brushed mine, hesitantly at first, and then more sure.

For the first time in forever, I didn't even think. I didn't worry about the trances; I didn't worry about the numbers. I kissed him back. All that mattered at that moment was Jake and me, together. I wrapped my arms around his waist and cuddled close, letting my eyes drift shut. I did have a fleeting thought that this is not what I had resolved to do. In fact, it was the polar opposite. But I didn't want the night to end. Even though I knew it would have to.

I woke with Jake's arm still around me, my head still resting on his shoulder. I sighed contentedly and was about to nuzzle closer to him when I opened my eyes enough to see the angle of the sun coming through the windows. I bolted straight up on the couch. It was morning. We must have fallen asleep during the second movie. I checked my watch. 7:05. Dad would be coming home soon.

"Jake," I whispered. I shook his arm. "Wake up."

His eyes opened slowly, reluctantly. And then sprang open wide.

"It's morning," I said needlessly.

"Oh, man!" He jumped to his feet. "I'm sorry. I should . . . get going."

"Right."

In the hallway, he bent to pull on his boots. "I left my bike at the mall," he called over his shoulder. "Could you give me a ride? I'm supposed to be playing for a church group in an hour."

"Oh." My stomach sank. "I . . . don't drive."

He paused and looked back at me. "Seriously?"

"It's a long story."

When Jake stepped into the bathroom to put on his shirt and tie, I grabbed my cell phone and dialed Michelle. She was understandably suspicious, but I promised I would explain everything after we dropped Jake off at the mall. I felt like a middle schooler, having to make arrangements for a boy to be picked up from my house.

The ride to the mall was awkward at best. I hadn't thought to ask Jake how he would feel about Michelle providing the transportation and he looked shocked and more than a little embarrassed when she showed up. I kept apologizing and he kept telling me it was okay. Michelle drove without a word, although her eyebrows kept rising and rising until I thought they would disappear into her hairline.

As soon as we left him in the parking lot, she turned to me, her eyes almost as huge as her smile. "Okay," she demanded. "You have to tell me *everything*!"

"Seriously," I told her. "Nothing happened. We fell asleep watching TV."

"Why did he leave his bike here? How did he think he was going to get home?"

I told her how he had run after me, literally, and she clutched her chest. "That is so *romantic*!"

"It's not like that," I told her. "We're just friends."

She didn't believe me, but I hadn't really expected her to.

"Tell me about the meet," I said. "How did you do?"

"I'll tell you." She lowered her sunglasses and gave me a look over the tops of them. "But this conversation is not over. I want you to know that."

For the next twenty minutes, we drove around town while she recounted the events of the day I'd missed. Surprisingly, I felt only mild disappointment that I hadn't been there.

"I'd better get home," I said finally. "My dad's coming back today."

"All right." She turned the car around. "But we need to meet up later because you owe me details!"

Michelle dropped me off at the curb. Across the street,

Mrs. Briggs stood at her open front door instead of in her window. She looked me over and pressed her lips together in a prim line. I could almost hear her *hmmph* as she raised her nose in the air and turned to go inside her house.

I trudged up to the front door. What was *that* about? I pulled out the key to let myself in the house, but when I grabbed the handle, the door opened. Unlocked.

Uh-oh.

17

"Dad?" I called. "Are you home?"

From the back of the house I heard angry footsteps and I held my breath, wishing I could duck back outside.

"Ashlyn," Dad's voice demanded. "Front and center."

I made the prisoner's walk to the great room, averting my eyes from my mom's room on one side and the living wall on the other. Dad stood waiting for me in a classic anger pose: elbows out at sharp angles, chest puffed up, chin thrust forward.

"How was your trip?" I asked weakly.

"How was your weekend?" he countered.

I sighed and walked over to the kitchen table, pulled out a chair. I didn't have the energy to deal with a whole roundabout line of questioning. I wished he'd just say what he wanted to say to me and get it over with. I sat.

"Where were you just now?" he asked.

"With Michelle. We were driving around, talking."

He nodded, but briskly, dismissively, as if this was not the information he was after. "Mrs. Briggs reported that you were entertaining boys in the house. Could you explain that, please?"

Mrs. Briggs. I should have known. "Not boys, Dad," I shot back. "One boy. One. I don't know what she means by 'entertaining' either. We were watching a movie and we fell asleep. That's it."

"You know the rules, Ashlyn. No friends in the house while I'm gone."

"We didn't plan it. He was walking me home and we got caught in the rain and—"

"Rules are rules. I need to know that I can trust you."

"Of course you can, Dad. Haven't I—"

"I don't know, Ash." He blew out a heavy breath. "Ever since you went back to that mall job, you haven't been yourself. Skipping school, missing meets, disregarding the rules . . . I think it's best you quit now before things go any further."

"Quit working?" I stared at him, stunned. "That job has nothing to do with—"

"Yes. Now. Today. As of this moment, you are done."

I shot up from my chair. "No! I can't leave them shorthanded this week. It's—"

His face grew red and he raised his voice. "This is not open for discussion, Ashlyn. You've chosen this course by your actions. Our arrangement isn't working out any longer."

I took a step back. "What do you mean?"

"A guardian," he said. "Someone to watch over you while I'm away. Mrs. Briggs said that she would be willing to come over and—"

"What? You've got to be kidding."

"Why? She's close, she's reliable. She can stay here with you."

"I don't need a babysitter, Dad."

He folded his arms. "I don't know *what* you need, Ashlyn. But I'm not going to stand by and let you jeopardize everything you've worked so hard to accomplish by being reckless. I won't stand by and let you throw your dreams away by—"

"Your dreams."

"What?"

"*Your* dreams. You have no idea what mine are."

His voice dropped. "Excuse me?"

I just about backed down, but enough was enough. I had to stand up to him and he had to hear it. "This is about what *you* want, Dad. But I'm not a perfect student and I'm not the track star you want me to be, okay? I don't even like track. I run because I want to. On my own, not to compete. I run because you used to run with me. Why don't we do that anymore?"

His face turned red and he turned away.

"You thought ShutterBugz would be good for me," I continued. "You *wanted* me to work there. But now that you don't want that for me anymore, I'm just supposed to quit?"

"We are not discussing this right now, Ashlyn."

I slammed the chair I had been sitting on up against the table. "So when, Dad? When I'm dead like Mom? When I'm gone like Kyra? When do you intend to *talk* to me?"

He wouldn't even look in my direction. "That's enough," he said, and retreated to his office.

"You can't hide in there forever!" I yelled after him.

But the sad thing was, I knew he could.

To my surprise, Dad actually joined me at the table that afternoon instead of asking me to bring his lunch into the office.

He ate politely, napkin in his lap, elbows tucked close to his side, offering appropriate thanks and compliments at appropriate times. For a minute, I thought that his anger from that morning was forgotten. But when he was done, he laid his fork carefully across his plate and cleared his throat. "Ashlyn," he said, "I've asked Mrs. Briggs to keep an eye on things while I'm gone tomorrow."

"What? Tomorrow? But—"

He raised his hand to shut me up. "She won't have to

come over, but you'll need to check in with her when—"

"No. I mean, you're leaving? It's not on the schedule."

"Emergency meeting. It couldn't be helped." He laid his napkin next to his plate and stood up from the table and that was the end of it.

I called Carole that afternoon to break the news about me quitting. I lied and said it had to do with school and that my dad wouldn't let me keep a job until I brought my grades up. I didn't see the point in letting her know that my dad stupidly believed her kiosk had anything to do with my troubles.

She responded in usual Carole fashion; denial, acceptance, and then panic. "No, that can't be. Oh, dear. We will miss you. What are we going to do without you this week?" She promised that I could come back to work whenever I was ready, which made me feel even worse about abandoning her.

I hung up with Carole and was just about to call Michelle when the familiar buzz began to gather in the back of my head.

Grabbing a notebook from my backpack, I hurried over to the desk and sat, flipping through the pages to the first blank space I could find. I picked up a pen and dared the vision to show itself.

The effect was immediate. Before I even felt the pen touch the paper, the room disappeared. Wind rushed in my ears and I found myself in the dark, standing alone on a long stretch of highway.

> *In the distance, bright beams of headlights speed toward the boy in the road. He doesn't see them. I panic and rush to one side of the road and then the other, trying to get his attention. I don't know where to tell him to go to get out of the way. I reach for him, but before I can touch him, I feel myself being sucked away.*

I came to with my head on the desk, the walls swirling around me like a vortex. Bolting upright, I pressed the pencil to the paper again. *Come on. Please.* I needed more. I needed to see his face.

But no matter how I tried, I couldn't go back. The trance was over.

Mrs. Briggs came over before Dad left the next afternoon and he gave her a whole list of instructions. I had to leave the room because I couldn't stand the pleased pinch to her lips now that she knew she was really in charge. At least he wasn't going to make me stay with her, but still.

I hid in my room and felt pretty sorry for myself, watching another day slip into evening. And then Michelle knocked on my bedroom window. I scrambled over my bed and let her in.

"Put on your shorts," she said. "We're going running."

"What? But we went this morning."

She crossed to the closet. "Don't argue. Where are those cute blue shorts with the hearts on them?"

"Since when do you care what I—"

She silenced me with a look. "Get dressed," she said.

I understood the reason for the running, of course. It's so I could escape from the house without Mrs. Briggs saying anything. But Michelle was up to something, I could feel it.

We started out on our regular route, but instead of turning left when we got to Earlington, we turned right, toward the park.

"Okay, I give up," I said. "What are we doing?"

Michelle did a little skip for a few steps. "I know someone who's anxious to see you," she sang.

I couldn't help but smile. "Jake?"

She nodded. "I ran into him yesterday when I went to the mall to grab some eyeliner at Sephora, and he asked for your phone number. Seems you guys never got around to sharing contact information, huh? So I got you his, too." She handed me a slip of paper, grinning so hard I thought her cheeks would break. "You can thank me later. Anyway, he said he hoped he'd see you at work, but then when he found out you quit . . ."

I practically turned cartwheels right there.

"They're supposed to meet us by the parking lot."

"They?"

"Trey and Jake. You didn't think I would miss this reunion, did you?"

When I saw Jake ahead, I was glad that Michelle had talked me into primping. He looked achingly wonderful in his basketball shorts and a sleeveless Under Armor tee that showed off his biceps. His boots had been replaced by a pair of black high-tops. He was leaning up against a silver Mazda, talking to Trey, one arm slung casually over a basketball, but when he saw us, he pushed away from the car and waved. His smile sent warm chills through me.

I was so happy to see Jake that I didn't even mind the self-satisfied smiles Michelle kept throwing at me. Or when she announced that she had to get home to pack for South Carolina and asked Trey if he would mind going with her. It was all so un-smooth that I probably should have been embarrassed. But I wasn't.

Jake and I played basketball for a while, then we wandered around the grounds until we ended up at the playground. I had forgotten the simplicity and joy of playground equipment. We climbed up on the slide and slid down, ran in circles at the merry-go-round, hung upside down on the jungle gym, and tried to out-pump each other on the swings, seeing which one of us could go higher. On the playground, I had the power to do whatever I wanted. I could go as high or as fast as my own strength would allow. It was the first time in a very long time that I felt completely free.

"I brought something to show you," Jake said as we walked back toward the parking lot. "Come on." He took my hand and held it the rest of the way.

He opened up the trunk of the Mazda and took out an old, beat-up guitar case. "This," he said, "is the first guitar I ever owned." He closed the trunk again and led me over to a bench nearby. We sat and he unfastened the silver clasps to open the case. Inside lay an old acoustic steel-string guitar. He picked it up gently and rested the body snug against his knee.

"I was thinking," he said as he adjusted the tuning pegs. "After you showed me your photography, I should show you what I love to do." He strummed a couple of chords and then adjusted the pegs again, then took the pick in his hand and looked up at me with little-boy earnestness. "Don't laugh."

If seeing him at the piano was revelation, seeing Jake with a guitar in his hands was pure magic. He started slow, coaxing sweet, simple notes from the strings, and then the tempo changed and the music took over. His fingers danced over the frets to a song I'd never heard before. It tugged at my chest, made me want to cry.

When he finished, he looked up at me shyly. "So . . . that's what I do."

"It's wonderful."

He shrugged. Thunder rumbled in the distance and he glanced up at the sky. "We'd better get you home if we don't want a repeat performance of the other night."

I laid my hand over his. "Jake, thank you."

His smile surfaced again. "You're welcome."

18

The next day, Michelle dropped by to see if I wanted to see a movie. I didn't even have to think about that one. I grabbed my purse and ran out the door.

"You look pretty dressed up for a movie." I slid into the passenger seat and buckled my seat belt. "What are we doing?"

"Smile and wave," Michelle said.

"What?"

"Smile. And. Wave." She gestured with her head to where Mrs. Briggs stood watching from her picture window. "Unbelievable. Does she ever take a break?"

"Just get me out of here," I said.

She couldn't keep from smiling.

"So, where are we really going?" I asked.

Michelle shrugged. "Just one more innocent gathering

before I take off for South Carolina tomorrow. We're having lunch at La Scala."

La Scala was one of the nicer restaurants at the mall. But it could have been McDonald's for all I cared. All that mattered is that I was going to see Jake again.

The guys were waiting for us at a corner booth when we got there. Jake looked up and smiled and a warm shiver ran down my spine. I noticed that he wasn't wearing his ugly music-note tie, and hoped that meant he wasn't working and this wasn't just his break. That way, we'd have more time together.

I slid onto the seat next to him. "Hey, stranger."

"How've you been?"

"Okay. How about you?"

He smiled at me. "Never better."

I can't even remember what I ate that day. All I could think about was that Jake was there with me. He held my hand and I could barely follow the conversation. But when Michelle and Trey started talking about the next track meet, my ears perked up.

"Saint Mary's is a tough team," Trey said. "Inner city. You don't want to mess with those guys."

"Remember last year at the basketball play-offs, we had to have a police escort to get out of the arena?" Michelle shuddered at the memory. "You don't think we'll have anything like that at the meet, do you?"

"Nah," Trey said. "Track's not as big a sport at their school."

"But I thought you said we had to watch out."

"Yeah." He shrugged. "For the team, not the school. They're mean, I'm tellin' you. These guys will do anything to win: dope up, intimidate, play dirty. They even have to do random drug testing for all their meets because they were suspended from competition a few years ago."

At the mention of drugs, Michelle glanced up at me for just a moment too long. I shifted uncomfortably and she turned her attention back to Trey. "Do both teams have to be tested, or just Saint Mary's?"

I took a sip of water to hide my humiliation. She probably couldn't help thinking about how she had found me wasted just the week before. My face burned at the memory. It wasn't one of my proudest moments.

The waitress stopped by the table to "make sure our dining experience had met with our expectations," which, in waitress speak, meant that we had occupied her table long enough and it was time to order dessert or leave. We left.

Michelle and Trey made another smooth getaway and Jake offered to take me home. I felt like I was walking on top of the world. Until we returned to the car.

Jake didn't talk at all as he drove, but the way he kept drumming his thumbs against the steering wheel, I knew he wanted to say something.

"What is it?" I coaxed.

I had been hoping he wanted to tell me how much he liked me or that he'd had a great time or something like that, but when he turned to me, his face told a different story. My heart dropped.

"This is . . . difficult for me," he said.

Great, I thought. *He's just not that into me. He has a girlfriend. He's moving to Antarctica.*

"Can I be honest with you?"

I frowned. "Of course."

"I'm . . . worried about you."

I went stiff. Not him, too. "Do I dare ask why?"

He drummed the steering wheel again. "Are you . . . using something?"

"Using?"

"Yeah. I mean, like . . ." He cleared his throat. "This is hard."

"Go on," I said icily. "Nothing but the truth."

"That night I first saw you—you were acting . . . kind of strung out. And when I was at your house, you seemed anxious. Jumpy."

"Anxious?"

He nodded. "And then you went back into your room and after you came back, you got really relaxed."

"And to you, this means I'm *using*."

"Not until I saw the look Michelle gave you when they were talking about drug testing. And how you reacted."

"Oh, really. And how did I react?"

He looked me in the eye. "Like you know you have a problem."

Yes I did; the kind of problem I could never tell him about. I stared out the window. "I don't expect you to understand."

"Then explain it to me because I really *don't* understand. It's self-destructive and stupid. What would you do if they *did* test you for drugs and find out you're using?"

I folded my arms tight across my chest and glared at him. "You don't know what you're talking about."

"But I do know. I've seen it. I know what addiction can do to you. What it can take away from you."

"Oh. So now I'm addicted? Well, thank you for your insight, but it isn't what you think."

He gave me a look as if to challenge me to tell him what it was he thought, and I hated him for it. I hated the mixture of pity and disgust I saw in his eyes—as if I was some junkie who didn't understand what was wrong with her. Thing was, I knew. And it had nothing to do with pills. I folded my arms. "Pull over."

"What?"

"I said, pull over. Now, please."

"Ashlyn . . ."

"Please."

He flicked the blinker and pulled onto the shoulder, rolling slowly to a stop. "What's the—"

I wrenched open the door and jumped out. "Good-bye, Jake."

"Ashlyn, come on."

I slammed it on his protests.

"Don't go," he called, but his voice was muffled through the glass.

For an instant, looking at the way his eyes pleaded with me, I almost changed my mind. But if he thought he was disappointed in me now, what would he think if he learned the truth? I started walking.

Behind me, his door creaked open. "Ashlyn."

I began to run. There would be no good outcome for this conversation. I knew that. He was going to believe whatever he was going to believe, and I couldn't tell him otherwise. What would I say? That I was a transcriber for the divine? He might as well think I was a junkie. At least that was believable.

The door slammed and his boots pounded the pavement as he came after me. I cut off to my right, climbing up the steep embankment and then ran into the woods. I could hear him huffing up the hill behind me. "Ashlyn! Wait!"

But all I wanted at that moment was to run as fast and as far as I could—away from him, away from home, away from the trances. It was too hard. Too much. I didn't want to deal with it anymore.

I tore past the trees, ducking under branches, slapping

them away. The smell of pine tar clung to my hands, my clothes. Under my feet, the ground swelled and dipped so that it felt like I was running on a rolling ship.

I ran until I thought my legs would collapse beneath me, until my lungs felt tight and raw—and then I ran some more. I could hear Jake crashing through the trees behind me, but he couldn't catch me. That was when I was glad to have worked so hard at conditioning. For one brief moment I felt powerful. In control. But that moment quickly passed like a burst of flame from a match. In control was exactly what I was not. Not even close.

And Jake knew it.

"Ashlyn! Wait!" he called.

When I couldn't run anymore, I finally turned to face him, gulping in air. I bent at the waist, resting my hands on my knees as I tried to catch my breath. Strangely, it was harder now that I had stopped than it was when I was running.

"Why?" I wheezed.

"Why . . . what?" He was as out of breath as I was. Maybe more.

"Why do you even care?" I straightened and pushed my shoulders back, my chin at a defiant angle that was supposed to show more confidence than I felt. "What is it to you?"

He spread his hands out before him. I didn't know if it was a gesture of confusion or surrender. "Look, I'm sorry if

I . . ." He drew in a breath. ". . . crossed the line back there. I didn't mean to upset you."

That wasn't an answer. I stared him down, challenging.

"It's just that . . ." He paused and cleared his throat. "You're a good friend, and . . ." He shook his head. "No, that sounds stupid. I'm not good at this."

I folded my arms. "Good at what? What are you trying to do?"

For just an instant he met my eyes, then looked away again. "I really like you," he said in a gruff voice, as if it made him mad or something.

"Why?" I asked once more, but less demanding this time.

"You're different," he said.

I scoffed. He had no idea what an understatement that was.

"I mean that in good way." He assured me. "I don't know. I just . . . I care what happens to you."

For the longest time, we just stood there, me staring at him, him staring at me. Unlike most of the guys I knew from school, he wasn't afraid to look me straight in the eye when he said something like that. But then it felt like he was looking through my eyes, deep inside of me, so I slammed down the shades before he could see too much.

"You . . . don't have to worry," I said, turning away. *Tell him what he wants to hear.* "I'll be fine."

"Wait, Ashlyn." He took my hand and tried to tug me back toward him again. "I'm just trying to tell you that I understand. I'm here for you."

I resisted his pull.

"You think I don't get it, but I do," he said quietly. "My brother was an alcoholic. I know addictive behavior."

"But I'm not—"

"Oh, come on, Ashlyn. It's me. Nothing but the truth, remember?"

I spun to face him. "You're not *interested* in the truth. You've already made up your mind that you know what's wrong with me, but what you think is so far from the truth it's not even—"

"So tell me, Ashlyn. Let me help."

I deflated. What was I to him, a charity case? I pulled my hand away. "I don't need your *help*, Jake."

He sighed. "That's not what I meant."

We stood looking at each other for a long time. "I was in an accident, okay?" I said finally. "Last fall. I broke my back and the doctors didn't even know if I was going to walk again."

"That must have been really painful."

"More than you'll ever know."

"Is it pain meds?"

My hands curled into tight fists. "Are you even *listening* to me?"

He stepped away from me. "It tore me up, watching my

brother's addiction destroy his life." He looked to me with sad eyes. "I can't do that again. I won't. But I'll always be here for you, Ashlyn. Let me know when you want to talk." And with that, he turned and walked away.

He didn't look back.

After Jake left, I wandered back through the woods to the road, but his car wasn't there. I hadn't really expected him to wait for me, but my chest grew tight just the same when I saw he was gone. By then, the sun sat just beyond the tree line, glowing hot orange and pink behind the branches. It threw long shadows like skeletal claws that stretched across the pavement.

Shoving my hands into the pockets of my jacket, I began to walk. I seethed inside, remembering everything Jake had said, the assumptions he made. He wouldn't even *listen* to me!

But then I had to admit that the first time since I can remember, someone had recognized there was something wrong with me, but instead of running away, he wanted to get closer. Someone actually cared for me enough to stick around.

If only I could fool myself into thinking it would be the same if he knew what a mess I was. And I was a mess. I'd been holding my secrets inside for so long, I had lost all sense of perspective. I needed to find myself again. I needed to talk it out, but the only person who really understood me—because she shared the same secrets as I did—didn't want to talk to me. Who else did I have?

There was only one other person—besides Jake—who I could trust to be completely honest with me. I walked back to the mall, hoping Gina was working that night. She'd probably just tell me to get over it, but maybe that's what I needed to hear.

If she was surprised to see me, you would never know from looking at her. She just glanced up from the magazine she was reading and said, "So you don't hate this mall as much as you thought, huh?"

Despite myself, I smiled. "How's it going tonight? Slow?"

She closed the magazine and leaned back against the counter. "That's not why you're here."

For a moment, I almost lost my nerve, so I just blurted it out before I could change my mind. "How do you convince someone you're sorry for something terrible you've done?"

Her eyebrows raised a notch. "Well. This should be an interesting conversation." She pushed off the stool, pausing a moment to redistribute her weight, and then waddled to the back section of the kiosk. "Come into my office. Let's talk."

She sat on one of the studio chairs and motioned for me to take a stool. "Now," she said, "why don't you tell me what this is about?"

I sat and picked at the lint on the table drape. "It's my fault my mom died," I said.

Her expression didn't change, but she shifted in her seat. "I see. How did it happen?"

"Car accident. I was driving."

"Ouch. Harsh."

"I know. My sister can't bring herself to talk to me. She moved away before I even got out of the hospital. And my dad . . ."

"Ah." Her voice became serious. "I'm sure they know how sorry you are, Ashlyn. You just have to be patient. Everyone has their own process of handling grief."

"It's more than that. I . . . I have visions."

"Flashbacks of the accident?"

"Not exactly." I picked up a stuffed-lamb prop and ran my fingers through its acrylic fleece. "More like premonitions."

"Whoa."

Once I got started, I couldn't stop. I told Gina everything—the trances, the night at the party.

"And the writing? The numbers? That's the catalyst?"

"Yes," I said.

"That's about the coolest thing I've ever heard."

"Cool?" I jumped up from the stool. "Are you kidding me? How can you even—"

"Oh, come on. Sit down. I apologize for my bad choice of words. It's *fascinating*. You have a gift."

"Some gift," I muttered.

"Everything has a purpose, Ashlyn. It's up to you to discover what it is." She sat back and studied me. "But . . . that's not what you want to hear right now. So out with it. Tell me the rest."

I hesitated for an instant. "Okay, here's the thing; I really like someone, and—"

"Jake."

I nodded miserably.

She laughed. "Like I didn't see that one coming. If it makes you feel any better, he has it bad for you, too. I can tell by the way he watches you, like he's in pain or something. It's kinda sweet. You should tell him how you feel and put him out of his misery."

"I think he pretty much knows by now," I mumbled.

For the first time since I'd met her, Gina looked truly surprised. "By now?" she repeated. "I must be losing my touch. What did I miss?"

I told her about the night Jake spent at my house, the movies, the kiss. How I had been sneaking out from under Mrs. Briggs's watchful eye to meet him.

She shifted on her chair. "Well. You have been busy. I

can see I need to reset my radar. So what's the problem?"

"The problem is, Jake doesn't know about the trances. He thinks I've been acting weird because I'm on drugs or something. I'm afraid if I tell him . . ."

"Oooh. I see." She rubbed both hands absently over her belly. "You'd rather he think you're a stoner. You don't trust him enough to be your friend if he knows the big, bad truth about you."

I had to admit, it sounded pretty lame the way she put it. But I had tried to explain it to him once and he wouldn't listen. "He's going to believe what he wants to believe. Trying to explain would only make it worse."

"Oh, give me a break. Even you don't believe that load of crap. Look, Ashlyn, there's no substitute for honesty. Not everyone has to know every detail of your life, but this is Jake we're talking about. He's good people. You're not doing yourself any favors by shutting him out. Tell him the truth."

"Didn't you say that sometimes people are more important than the truth?"

"I was talking about protecting feelings, not keeping secrets."

"But what if he—"

She pushed herself to her feet. "Respect him enough to find out." She nudged me as she passed on her way back up to the front. "And there's no time like the present."

I turned around and my stomach did a complete

somersault when I saw Jake, shoulders bowed, walking toward the kiosk. Gina waved to him, her bracelets jangling. "Hey, sweetie! How's it going?"

"Not so good. I could really use someone to talk—" He stopped dead in his tracks when he saw me sitting there.

Gina leaned her elbows on the counter. "Oh, I'm sorry, hon, I'm really busy. But I'm sure Ashlyn would be happy to talk to you." She turned and gave me a pointed look. "Wouldn't you, Ashlyn?"

I stood shakily, rubbing my palms against the legs of my pants. "Yeah. I really would."

Looking back, I wonder what might have happened if Jake had turned and walked away. If I had listened to the warning bells clanging inside my head as his eyes met mine. Both of us had plenty of time to back out as the silence stretched between us, but neither one of us did.

Nothing about Jake's dour expression or the way he stood with arms crossed tight across his chest said that he was interested in what I had to say, but at least he didn't leave. That was something. I swallowed my hesitation and slipped out from behind the kiosk counter.

As I stood in front of him, my words got lost. How could I expect him to understand unless I told him everything? And I couldn't do that if he was going to just walk away from me again. I had to know that he would stick around long enough to listen.

So I slugged his arm.

"Ow!" His eyes widened in surprise.

"That was for leaving me," I said, and stalked past him.

It didn't take long before he fell into step beside me, rubbing his biceps. "I didn't know what else to do."

"Then you shouldn't follow me now," I said, "because it doesn't get any easier."

"I know."

I shot him a sideways glance. "You really don't know anything."

He grabbed my hand and pulled me to a stop. "Then tell me. I promise to listen this time."

I looked back over my shoulder to the kiosk, where Gina stood watching. She made big sweeping gestures with her arms and mouthed, "Go on."

I took a deep breath and turned my attention back to Jake. "Can we go someplace and talk?"

We sat at one of the deserted tables in the food court. It was late enough that we had the whole back corner to ourselves. For what seemed like a very long time, we just sat and looked at each other before Jake finally spoke.

"Ashlyn, you can tell me anything. Everything."

I traced the pattern of the wood grain on the table with my finger. "It's hard."

"Doesn't have to be. We just decide right now. You be

completely open with me, I'll be completely open with you. And no one walks away. Deal?"

His eyes held mine.

"Deal," I said softly.

He nodded grimly, and I realized for the first time that being open could be as hard for him as it was for me. He squared his shoulders and cleared his throat. "I'll start, okay?"

I nodded.

"When I was growing up, my brother was my idol. He's four years older than I am and I always wanted to be just like him. He was smart. Funny. Good at sports. Everyone liked him. And then . . ." He stared at his hands on the table, his voice growing quiet. "In high school, he started to act different, like he was a stranger in my brother's body. I never knew what was coming when he was around. One day he'd be completely normal, and the next, he was mean and bitter. He'd throw things around, punch holes in the drywall. He was holding so much anger inside he had to hit something just to let it out."

His hand drifted up to his forehead and he fingered the scar absently. He'd said he got the scar wrestling with his brother. Suddenly, I understood. They hadn't been wrestling for fun.

"Jake, stop. You don't have to tell—"

"Yeah, I do." He reached across the table and took my hand. "It's only fair."

I caught the corner of my lip between my teeth and stared at the way his fingers curled around mine. Strong. Sure. Everything I was not. After so many years of hiding the truth, I didn't know how I was going to be able to tell him what he wanted to hear. He was probably expecting some kind of confessional about how I got hung up on my meds, not a story about trances and visions. But when I looked into his eyes all I saw was trust.

"Okay," I whispered.

He nodded and his thumb rubbed back and forth over my knuckles as we sat still at the table, talking with our eyes. Finally, Jake drew a breath to speak again. "At first I tried to cover for him. I didn't want my mom and dad to see what was happening with him." His words were rushed, like he needed to get them out. "But then when he got caught, I'd get in trouble, too, for being an accomplice." He looked down at our hands. "And I guess I was. By trying to protect him, I just helped him get worse."

"You didn't know," I offered.

He accepted that with a shrug. "That's not the bad part. I . . . started to hate my brother. Started to resent cleaning up his messes. For years I've been trying to make it easier on my mom and dad by being everything he could have been. I got good grades, lettered in baseball, picked up the slack. But they—" He cleared his throat. "I don't think they've ever even noticed. My brother's drinking took over everything until they didn't see me anymore."

I dropped my eyes to the table. I knew what it was like to be lost behind the bigger problem.

"He's in prison now," Jake continued in a low voice, glancing around like he was afraid someone else might hear. "DUI and vehicular homicide."

Cold washed over me. I heard the screeching of tires, crumpling of metal. Felt the pain all over again. Another crash. Another drunk driver. I hated the driver in our accident for taking my mom away. Almost as much as I hated myself.

"I'm sorry," I murmured.

"That's why I work at Kinnear. My mom and dad couldn't afford the attorney fees, so Uncle Dale loaned them the money on the condition that I work it off in the store."

"That's not fair."

Jake shrugged. "Life isn't fair."

I knew that was true.

"So," he concluded, "now you know. That's who I am."

"No." I held Jake's eyes with mine. "It's what happened. Not who you are."

He nodded slowly and his grip on my hand tightened. "Now it's your turn. What happened with you?"

I chewed my lip again. Would he understand? *Respect him enough to find out*, Gina had said. I took a deep breath. "I have visions," I said.

Once I started talking, everything tumbled out in one long stream. After so many years of keeping it all inside, it felt good to confide in someone else. Gina was like a warm-up. Jake got the full treatment. To his credit, he didn't freak out or run away, even though I could tell by the way his eyes got wider and wider that he was more than a little bit shocked by what he was hearing. But he just nodded the whole time, holding my hand in both of his and encouraging me to continue if I faltered or my words trailed off.

"So that's my life. It's not pretty, but there's not a whole lot I can do about that."

"I don't know. I always heard that if you don't change the things you don't like, you have no one to blame but yourself."

I snorted. Suddenly, he sounded like one of my counselors. "Oh really? Then what about you?"

"Me?"

"Right. Hanging out in your brother's shadow, apologizing for him, trying to clean up his messes. You don't belong in that music store, and you know it. I've seen you in there. It's like watching a wild animal in a cage."

Jake looked away. "Yeah, well, once Uncle Dale has his money—"

"But it isn't your responsibility. What would you rather be doing?"

He stared at me hard for a moment and then his mouth softened and he sighed. "For real?"

"For real."

"There's a local band that needs a guitarist for the summer tour. A couple of the guys came into the store the other day and they were talking about tryouts this weekend."

"See? That's what I'm talking about. You should go for it."

A smile touched his lips. I hoped that meant he was considering it. "How about we make a deal? I promise to try out if you get your license."

"Nice one, but I already have my license. I just don't drive. Not anymore."

"Let me see."

"What? You don't believe me?"

"I just want to see it, that's all."

I pulled back. "No way. It has the world's most terrible picture on it."

"It can't be that bad." He held out his hand.

I made a face. "Believe me; it is."

"Completely open," he reminded me.

I sighed and pulled my license out of my wallet.

Jake grabbed it, grinning in victory, but when he looked at it, the smile froze on his face. "It's not that bad," he said, forcing a cheerfulness that I knew he didn't feel.

My chest twisted in confusion. Jake was shutting down before my eyes. From what? Looking at my license? It didn't make sense. I shouldn't have told him about the visions. It must have been too hard after all. I should have—

Jake slid back into conversation like nothing was wrong, but I could feel him holding back, forcing his laughter. Finally, I stood. "I have to go," I said. "Thanks for talking with me."

As I feared, he didn't try to stop me, but looked up, distracted, like he had already moved on to the next thing on his list. "Yeah," he said. "I'll see you around."

I didn't hear from Jake the next day. Or the day after that. I kept turning on my cell phone just to make sure it was working. It was. I even pulled out the number Michelle had given me and texted him, but he never texted back.

It really should have come as no surprise. This is why I

never talked about myself. It was too much for people to handle, even people like Jake. After all his talk of honesty, I wanted to hate him for abandoning me like that, but I understood. He was just like everyone else.

I wandered through the empty house, feeling even emptier inside. I wanted it to end. I wanted to be normal. Whatever it took, I was going to complete the vision that kept repeating in my trances. Maybe then I would be free.

From what Gina said, all the numbers I wrote had energy, had vibrations. I could feel that in my head whenever the trances took over. I could also feel it whenever I stepped into my mother's parlor. As if her energy was still there.

I didn't believe what the church ladies said, that trance writing and the numbers were evil. But what if they were right about them being messages from the other side? That would account for the different handwriting. If my mom were there now, she would finally understand. She would want to help me. Slowly, barely breathing, I stepped into her room. The reaction was immediate. My heart raced, my hands turned cold, the buzzing in my head felt like it was going to make my brain explode. I must have been right, then. There was energy in that room.

The darkness had already started to gather by the time I felt my way to her writing table and sat down. I pulled a sheet of paper from the decorative stationery she never used and reached for a pen.

With a sudden *whoosh*, the room went dark.

***

I don't have time to think before a car races past me so close that the draft tosses my hair and sucks my breath right out of my lungs. I watch its headlights race ahead into the blackness, where another set of lights appear. I can feel my pulse hammering in my throat as the lights grow brighter, closer. And then the car swerves and loses control. A scream rises from me like the wail of a siren. I throw up my hands and wait for the impact, but it never comes.

Instead, numbers circle my head like huge crows, dipping, swooping, pecking at my brain as if to say that I should know what they mean. I try to wave them away, but my hands fly right through them. Fives, fours, nines . . .

Gina's voice floats above it all. You have the same number vibrations. The same vibrations. The same vibrations.

The numbers change into white lights. Car lights. Engines revving. Tires squealing. Speeding toward me. Speeding toward a boy in the road.

I scream. "Watch out!"

He turns to look at me and my stomach goes cold.

Jake?

The lights explode over my head and I feel myself falling backward.

***

When I came to, I was lying on my back on the floor, the chair to the desk on its side next to the wall. I sucked in a huge gulp of air, as if I had been underwater and had just now surfaced. The numbers. Where were the numbers?

I tried to push myself up, but the room was spinning, tilting, pieces settling into place. I rolled over onto my stomach and dragged myself to the desk, using it as leverage to haul myself up onto my knees. On the desk lay the stationery, bold numbers scrawled across it in masculine handwriting.

$$1+1+2+5 = 9$$
$$1+5+4+5+2+3+7+5 = 32$$
$$3+2 = 5$$

There were more numbers beneath, but the top line is all I needed to see. I recognized the configuration from when Gina did our numbers. When she pointed out that Jake's number vibrations and my own were the same. It only verified what I already knew from seeing his face in the trance.

Jake was the guy in the vision.

A wave of nausea rolled through my stomach but I fought against it. I didn't have time to be sick. Something bad was going to happen to Jake. I needed to see more. I needed more information so I could warn him.

I tried to right the chair I had knocked over, but it felt like rubber in my hands. Every time I set it on its feet, it fell over again. I finally decided I didn't have time to mess with it and grabbed the pen once more.

In an instant, I was back on the road, my head buzzing and twitching like a hundred live wires were jumping around in my brain.

Headlights sweep along the road, headed straight for me. I duck my head and suddenly I'm standing on the gravel shoulder, watching them race nearer. Jake is in the spot where I had been just a moment ago. I can see terror in the tenseness of his posture, the way he jerks this way and then that, not knowing where to stand to be safe. And then I see the Indian. Jake is straddling his bike. The car horn blares. I scream for him to look out, but in that instant, the car whizzes by—and then Jake is gone.

I must have jerked myself out of the trance again because all of a sudden the darkness dissolved and the pain in my fingers registered. "No!" I cried. "Where's the rest of it? That wasn't enough! I need to know where this happens! I need to know when!"

I pressed the tip of the pen to the paper again, but nothing happened. Frantic, I threw that piece of stationery behind me and grabbed another. I dug in the narrow drawer for a different pen to use. Nothing. I tried again and again and again, but I didn't even get a twinge.

The pen rolled from my fingers. I dropped my head to the desk and sobbed. How could this be it? After years of seeing visions I didn't want, now that I needed one to show itself, I get nothing?

I knew what Gina would say. She'd tell me I had seen all I was meant to receive. That's just the way it was. And then she'd tell me to stop whining and she'd ask me what I was going to do next. I lifted my head and wiped my eyes. What *could* I do? Warn Jake? Warn him of what? I didn't know enough to tell him anything. Besides, he wouldn't believe it. He had taken off as soon as he found out about me. He thought I was a freak, just like everyone else did.

So I would just have to find out what was missing in the vision another way. I needed a time. A place. And if I couldn't see it myself, I had no choice. I had to find Kyra.

21

My hands shook as I dialed the phone. This time she wouldn't hang up. This time I'd make her listen. I pressed the phone to my ear and my chest felt heavier with each ring that hummed from the other end of the line. And then a voice came on.

"We're sorry. You have reached a number that is no longer in service. If you think you have reached this recording in—"

"No. Please, no," I whispered, and dialed the number again.

"We're sorry. You have—"

I hung up and slumped to the floor with the phone in my hands. Did she want to avoid me so much that she had disconnected her phone after the last time I called? Then she left me no choice. I'd just have to go to wherever she was. I'd appeal to her in person so she couldn't run away. Then she would have to listen.

I dialed the phone again and listened to the faraway ringing. Finally, he picked up.

"Ben Greenfield."

"Dad?"

"Ashlyn?" His voice dropped low. "What is it? I'm in the middle of an important business din—"

"Dad, where's Kyra?"

The other end of the line went quiet. If it wasn't for the fact that I could still hear him breathing, I might have thought he'd hung up on me. "This is not a good time."

I closed my eyes and took a deep breath. "Where is she, Dad? I need to talk to her."

"Hold on." I could hear him making his apologies to whoever he was with, then heard a door open and close. "I am working, Ashlyn. We will discuss this when I get home."

"No! This can't wait." It was time to tell the whole truth, hold nothing back. No more pretending. I took a deep breath, hoping I was right. "Dad, listen to me. Kyra had a vision before Mom died. I should have seen it, too, but I had been drinking at that party and—"

"Ashlyn, stop."

"That's just it. I can't make the visions stop, Dad. I . . . I think I'm supposed to see them. And Kyra, too. But we can't do anything about them unless we work together." I wiped my eyes.

"Ashlyn, I told you—"

"I can't do this by myself. I need you to tell me where Kyra is. A friend of mine is in trouble and I need her to help me stop what I saw. Please. I'll take back everything I said before. I'll run track. I'll do whatever you want. Just tell me where she is so I can talk to her."

He was quiet again, and when he spoke, his voice sounded sad, old. "You don't have to be someone you're not to make me happy, Ash. That's not what I want for you."

I blinked away fresh tears, but I had to stay focused. "What about Kyra?"

"She's . . . not well."

"Where is she, Dad?"

His breath soughed through the phone line. "I'm coming home. I'll cancel the rest of the meetings. I can be there by—"

"I need to talk to her tonight. Now. Please, Dad. Tell me where she is."

He was quiet again. "Do you have a pencil?" he asked finally.

I grabbed the message pad from the counter. "Yes. I'm ready."

"I hope so, Ash," he said quietly. "You can find Kyra at the Gathering Place. 784 Sycamore Street. Ask at the desk. I'll call ahead and tell them it's all right."

"Tell who?"

But the line was dead.

***

The Gathering Place sounded familiar, but I couldn't remember why. I stared at the address on the message pad. 784 Sycamore. That was just across town. All this time, all this wondering . . . she'd been only twenty minutes away.

I grabbed the bus-route pamphlet from the basket on the counter and searched for the closest line that went to Sycamore. There wasn't one. There was a line that ran down Tara Hill, three blocks over, but the last run had been at 7:10. My hands turned to ice as I realized what that meant. If I wanted to get there tonight, I would have to drive. I hadn't been behind the wheel of a car since the accident. Just the thought of driving again made my stomach hurt, but I kept seeing Jake's face from the vision as he turned to look at me. I had to reach Kyra, no matter what it took.

I stood by the door to the garage for a long time, my hand on the doorknob, my chest hot and tight. The keys to the car still hung on the hook inside the little miniature cupboard my mom had gotten on one of her antiques shopping excursions. I couldn't bring myself to reach for them.

The insurance company had paid for a new car to replace the one that had been mangled in the accident. It sat in the garage, untouched. To use that car would have been like saying that everything could be put back the way it had been, but it couldn't. My mom was gone, and she was never coming back.

I squeezed my eyes shut tight and drew a deep, shaking breath. *She was never coming back.* It was time to let her go.

Before I could change my mind, I grabbed the keys from the cupboard and pushed outside into the garage. I walked toward the car slowly, carefully, like it was a wild animal that might bite if I startled it. My hands trembled as I opened the door, and when I slid into the seat and pulled on my seat belt, I felt like I had a tourniquet across my chest, squeezing, squeezing so tight I couldn't breathe. I put the key in the ignition and turned over the engine and pressed the garage door opener.

My entire body trembled so badly as I backed down the driveway that I had to stop the car and make myself breathe through it before I could go on. My hands were slick with sweat. I wiped them against my jeans and grabbed the steering wheel. This was something I could do.

Mrs. Briggs stood in her picture window, no doubt scandalized to see me leave without having checked with her first. I waved to her and drove away.

The last time I had seen Kyra, she'd been sitting on a chair in the corner of my hospital room. She wouldn't look at me. I wondered if she already knew then that she was going to go.

She did leave me a note. I found it when I came home from the hospital. She'd stuck it between the glass and the frame of our mirror so that only a corner of it was showing. I kept it, tucked into the bottom of the flowerpot. *I'm sorry*, it read. *It will be better this way.*

Better than what? I wondered. In all those weeks after my mom's funeral, we never *talked*. I never got the chance to tell her how sorry I was. I'd said the words, of course, over and over and over again. But I had never been able to bring myself to talk about that day, about what I had done. Then, once Kyra left, it was too late.

She'd given me no reason to hope that she would listen to me now, but what choice did I have?

I drove up and down Sycamore three times before I found the address. When my dad had said he was going to call "the desk," I pictured an apartment building or a dorm or something. In reality, 784 Sycamore was a house. Just a regular-looking house with a wraparound porch and a decorative wrought-iron fence out front. A sign in gilded lettering stretched over the front door: THE GATHERING PLACE.

I parked across the street and stared at the house for a minute, completely confused. And then I remembered where I'd heard of the Gathering Place. It was kind of like a halfway house for people with emotional and mental issues. Some kid from school had lived there for a while a year or so ago after he had tried to commit suicide. A sick feeling gripped my stomach as the reality I thought I knew slipped away. Dad said Kyra wasn't well. What had I been missing all these months?

Walking up to the door, I felt like I was moving through a dark dreamworld, the sidewalk stretching longer in front of me with every step, the door like a mouth opening to swallow me in the way it had Kyra.

"Hello," the woman at the door said cheerily. "You must be Ashlyn. We heard you were coming."

I couldn't answer, but let her usher me inside. A couple of girls glanced up from the board game they had spread on the floor between them. A guy in a chair laid down the book he was reading and watched us with open curiosity. It could have been any family room in any house—chairs and couches and potted plants tastefully arranged and framed pictures on the wall.

The woman, with her gauzy skirt and tunic-style blouse, was the only element that looked like it didn't belong with the family atmosphere and Victorian architecture. All she was missing was a chain of flowers in her hair.

"Some spring break, huh?" she said. "All this rain! At least the grass will be green."

She showed me to a rocking chair in the corner of the room and motioned for me to sit. I did, and she took the chair opposite. I noticed for the first time that she was wearing leather clogs with her earth mother ensemble.

Months ago, that was something Kyra and I would have laughed about. I wondered if we still could.

"We need to go over a few rules before we start," the woman said. "The Gathering Place is all about positive energy. If you've come to offer support to Kyra, wonderful! But we ask if you have any unresolved issues, you leave them outside. Can you do that?" She delivered her whole spiel in Disney mode, all smiles and bubbly inflection.

"Where is she?" I asked.

"I'm right here."

22

Kyra stood in the doorway, arms crossed tightly in front of her chest. She'd lost a lot of weight since she left; her cheeks looked hollow and the sweatshirt and pajama pants she was wearing hung on her like they were two sizes too big.

I stood. "Kyra."

She didn't move. "Why are you here?"

I slid a quick look at Earth Mother. She was watching raptly, eyes alight. I decided right then I didn't like her. "Is there someplace my sister and I can talk?" I asked. "In private?"

"Oh, we don't—"

"It's okay, Jane." Kyra pushed away from the doorframe. "We can talk in the library." Then her eyes went to me and she gestured with her head.

My chair rocked back as I stepped around Jane and hurried to follow Kyra. "Thanks," I called over my shoulder.

"Think positive!" Jane reminded.

The "library" was about the size of my mom's parlor and featured only one bookshelf that I could see. At least it was quiet and private. Kyra closed the door and turned to me. "How did you find this place?" she asked. "Why did you come?"

Now that I was in front of her, all the words I wanted to say fought to come out, but ended in a muddled heap in my head and all I could come up with was, "Why are *you* here?"

She didn't even answer, but crossed the room and stood in front of the window, staring out at the streetlight.

"Kyra," I said, "why are you living here? What's going on?"

"I don't expect you to understand." She turned to face me, arms folded across her chest again. I recognized it from all my therapy sessions as a self-protective gesture. My heart sank at the idea that Kyra felt she had to protect herself from me.

"I understand a lot," I said softly. "Try me."

She shook her head rapidly and stared up at the ceiling. "You can't be here," she said. "Don't you understand? We can't be together."

"Why?" I took a step toward her but she flinched and eyed the space between us, so I stopped.

She pulled the sleeves of her sweatshirt down over her hands and watched me, tears flooding her eyes. Her shoulders lifted and she shook her head. "I can't do it anymore, Ash. I . . . can't."

I didn't have to ask what she meant; I knew. I couldn't deal with the visions, either. "I understand."

"This place"—she looked around the room—"is perfect for someone like me. If they already think you're crazy, they don't ask a lot of questions."

"Except you're not," I said. "Come home with me."

"Is that why Dad sent you?" She narrowed her eyes. "To tell me to come home?"

"Dad didn't send me. I had to beg him for the address."

She turned away again. "You shouldn't have, Ash. You shouldn't have come. Don't you realize? With us both here together . . ."

"I know," I said. "That's . . . that's why I'm here."

"Then you might as well leave." She shook her head. "It's . . . too much." Her shoulders hunched and I realized she was crying.

I went to her then, touching her arm tentatively at first and when she didn't pull away, I laid a hand on her shoulder. "I know," I said again. "I've been . . . hiding from it, too."

"We can't help." She turned to me, eyes pleading. "Why do we have to see those things if we can't do anything to help?"

"Maybe we can."

She stepped back. "Oh, no. No. I told you. I can't do it anymore. Don't you get it? If I'm here, if we're apart, we can't complete the visions. We won't be responsible for anyone else getting hurt."

"But what if there's something we *can* do? I learned more about the numbers, Kyra. I learned how to make the trances start. If we—"

"No!" She pressed her hands over her ears and paced across the room. "I don't want to hear this."

"Please," I said, following her. "Just listen. We've never been able to change the events we saw before, so the trances kept coming. But I think there's a way we can make things right. I think if we can just complete this one vision and—"

"No."

"If we can do what we're meant to do, I think we can make them stop."

She shook her head.

"Kyra, please." We were both sobbing now. "I can't do this on my own. I need your help."

She stared at me as if I hadn't spoken.

I grabbed her arm and shook it. "It's a friend of mine, Kyra. Have you been seeing him, too? The guy on the motorcycle? I need to know what you saw, what you wrote. I need to warn him."

"I . . . haven't seen enough to help you."

"Then I need you to see it again. Any details you can remember, any hints—"

She pulled away from me and directed her stare across the room. "That's not how it works," she said. "We can't just summon a trance because we want to."

"But I *have*," I said. "Just focus on the energy and pick up the pen to write. I swear; it's that easy. But I can only see the part *I* was meant to see. We need to put the pieces together. Please, Kyra. This could be our chance to make things right."

Her eyes were haunted when she turned to me. "I just want it to end," she said.

"I know." I wrapped my arms around her the way she used to do with me for so many years. "I do, too."

We found a checkout slip and a pencil by the bookshelf. Kyra took them both to the coffee table and sat down before it, pencil in hand. And then we waited.

I sat on the arm of the sofa, hands clasped under my chin, and watched her. She stared at the paper, as if willing the message to appear on its own. For several minutes we sat like that and then she looked up at me. "It isn't working," she said.

"Don't give up," I pleaded. "Maybe start writing something and it will come."

She just stared at me like I was insane and I thought maybe she was going to argue with me again. Finally, though, she turned back to the desk and pressed her pencil to the paper. I peeked over her shoulder to see what she was writing, but it looked like nothing more than scribbles and scratches.

Then suddenly she stopped. Her shoulders tensed up and her posture went rigid. Her eyes rolled upward as the pencil began to move again. I held my breath. The trance had begun.

It was odd to see the writing from an outsider's perspective; I had always been the one writing. For the first time, I understood why my mom had been so upset about it as we grew older. I hate to use the word *creepy*, but the intensity of Kyra's movement paired with the blank look in her eyes came pretty close. Each number she wrote seemed to take intense effort to form. The point of the pencil pressed down so hard that it nearly tore through the paper. But slowly, slowly, I watched the numbers emerge.

And then, nothing. Her hand stopped moving. She lifted it from the page and then her whole body began to tremble.

"Gaah!" She came out of it like she had burst through a wall, throwing the pencil away from her and gasping like she'd just spent the last four minutes underwater.

"What?" I asked. "What happened?"

She turned her head slowly, her eyes coming into focus as they landed on my face.

"Kyra?"

Her expression never changed; it was like she was still in the trance, her face slack, eyes hollow. Still watching me, she stood.

"What is it?" I breathed.

She turned away, shaking her head.

"What?"

"It's over, Ashlyn." She stumbled toward the door and I ran behind her.

"Tell me," I begged. "What is it?"

She turned back to me, her eyes haunted. "You don't want to know," she said softly.

"Yes! Yes I do!"

She sagged against the doorframe. "It's bad, Ash."

A cold breath of fear raised the hairs on the back of my neck. "What did you see?"

"It's awful," Kyra whispered. "The worst vision I've ever seen. There's a crash. He's on a motorcycle. He doesn't stand a chance."

My face went numb. "No. Not if we stop it."

She just looked at me, her face pinched and wan. "Ashlyn, it's going to happen. There's nothing we—"

"No! We have to try! We have to change this. Tell me what you saw. Describe the road. I need to know every detail."

She took a deep breath like she needed extra strength

to speak. "It's dark. Nighttime. He's on a busy road; there are a lot of cars, going fast. Too fast for the rain. One of them spins out and another one hits it. Then another and another. He rides right into it, Ash. Right into the middle, just before the car behind him—"

"Rain?" I could barely speak. Her eyes followed mine out the window, where fat raindrops splattered against the glass. I looked again at the numbers she had written. By now I recognized his name. And something else. I counted the numbers out on the second line and my heart dropped. It matched the numeric equivalent of today's date. "It's happening tonight."

She nodded. "There's nothing we can do," she said again. "It's too late."

But I couldn't listen, couldn't accept what she was saying. I grabbed my cell phone from my pocket and desperately began punching in numbers. "We see events that are *going* to happen," I said. "It hasn't happened yet. We can still stop it." I may have been speaking to Kyra, but the words were mostly to myself. I wanted to believe it was true. I *had* to believe it was true.

The line on the other end began to ring and I pressed the phone to my ear. "Come on, Jake. Pick up!"

"Hey. It's me."

"Jake?"

"I can't get to the phone right now. You know the drill. *Beeeeep.*"

I hung up and dialed again.

"Hey. It's me."

And again.

"Hey."

"Ashlyn. Stop."

I clutched my phone to my chest, cupping both hands around it as if Kyra might try to make a grab for it. "No. There's still time. We have to at least try."

She closed her eyes and drew a deep breath. When she looked at me again, her face had changed. I wasn't sure what it was in the set of her jaw. Resignation maybe. Determination. Whatever it was didn't matter to me, so long as she would help. "Where is he?"

I stopped. "He works at the mall. He could be there."

"All right, then," she said. "Let's go."

I hesitated. "You're okay?" I asked. "I mean, you can just walk out, no questions asked?"

Kyra set her mouth in a grim line. "What do you think this is, a prison?"

"No! Of course not, but . . ." I thought of the guy from school who had lived at the Gathering Place, how he had been under a suicide watch. Seemed like they would keep close tabs on their residents. "I just thought—"

"Well don't. I can go wherever I want." She opened the door of the library and peeked out. "But let's steer clear of Jane, all right?"

***

I knew the minute I ran through Nordstrom that Jake wasn't working. Piano music drifted through the corridor from Kinnear music, but it wasn't Jake playing. The sound was too plinky, too soulless. Sure enough, as I got closer, I could see Uptight Suit Guy seated on the bench, back painfully straight, fingers curved like claws as he attacked the keys.

I swore and hitched my hands on my hips as I turned in a circle. What would I do now? Where could he be?

"Nice to see you, too," Gina called. She was seated on the stool behind the ShutterBugz counter, one of her ever-present magazines splayed open in front of her.

I ran over to the kiosk. "I'm sorry. I was just—"

"He came to talk to me, you know."

"Who?"

"Robert Downey Jr. Who do you think?" She blew out an impatient breath. "Jake."

I spun, looking for any sign of him. "When? Where is he?"

"He's not here, Ashlyn." She smoothed her hands over her belly and gave me a serious look. "But he said you guys had a good talk the other night."

"Yeah." I watched her cautiously. "We did."

"He, uh . . . Oooh!" Her face crumpled and she curled around her stomach, puffing in quick, short bursts.

"Are you okay?"

"Contractions," she panted. "Damn weather."

Now I was completely confused. "The weather?"

"Atmospheric changes," she said, straightening. "Gives me Braxton Hicks. You know, false labor? Baby's not due for another three weeks. I'd rather not do a dress rehearsal." She took one last deep breath and let it out in a long sigh. "Now, what were we saying?"

"Jake."

"Oh, yeah." Her voice sounded tight, like she didn't want to be the bearer of bad news.

I looked away from her so she wouldn't see the disappointment on my face. "It's okay, Gina. I know all that vision stuff was too weird for him to handle. But that's not what I came to—"

"It's not about the visions."

I met her eye. "It's not?"

"It's about the accident."

The wet road. Crashing metal. Shattering glass.

My knees felt weak. "He already knows?"

She looked at me strangely. "The driver. The one who hit your car . . ." She shifted on the stool again. "Jake didn't know until the other night."

My hands went cold. "Wait, what? *My* car?"

"It was his brother."

It felt like the ground opened beneath my feet. "What? What are you saying?"

"He figured it out when he saw the name on your license."

I blinked stupidly and gestured at Kinnear Music. "But . . . his name is Kinnear. His uncle—"

"Is his mom's brother." She leaned forward and placed her hand gently on mine. "Jake's last name is Anderson."

I pulled my hand away as if her touch burned. I couldn't breathe. That's how the numbers added up. Anderson. The name of the man in the headlines, the drunk who killed my mom. "I don't understand," I whispered. "Why didn't he tell me?"

"He wanted to."

"But?"

"He didn't know how. He's afraid you'll hate him. Like this was his fault or something."

I just kept shaking my head. This was all wrong.

"Now before you get upset, remember what I said about things happening for a reason. You getting transferred here, meeting Jake. He got you to open up, you got him to go for the audition and I think—"

My breath caught. "The what?"

"The audition tonight." She looked hopeful. "This could be a chance for both of you to move beyond—"

"That's where he's going!" I grabbed her arm. "Where is it?"

She pulled away, confused. "Where's what? The audition?"

I nodded breathlessly.

"Midland." She frowned. "Some club over—oh, merde. Here it comes again." Her hand flew to her belly and she bent over the counter, panting. "So what's up . . . with the . . . twenty questions . . . about Jake?"

I hesitated. But this was Gina I was talking to. She could handle it. "My sister and I saw Jake in a vision. I have to warn him."

She sprang straight up. "What? Why didn't you say . . . ugn!" Her face crumpled for a second. "No lie, this kid is going to . . . be an only child!" She grabbed the phone and started dialing.

"He's not picking up," I told her, but she had to hear for herself. She slammed the phone back down on the cradle. "Well, what are you standing around for? Go find him."

I hesitated. "What about you?"

"What about me?"

"The baby."

"Ashlyn, I swear . . ."

"I'm not going to leave you alone."

She gestured to the mall and the people around us. "I'm hardly alone."

"But if you need help—"

"It's false labor," she said between puffs of breath. "It'll go away. You, on the other hand . . ."

"Okay," I said. "I'm going, but I'll be back." I started to back out from behind the counter and she grabbed my arm.

"Wait," she wheezed. "Do you know where to look?"

I shook my head helplessly. "All I know is he's on a dark road. There are a lot of cars arou—"

"Enough." She lowered herself down from the stool. "I changed my mind. I'm coming with you. I don't know much, but I do know every road within a forty-mile radius of the mall. You describe it and I'll help you find it."

Lightning flashed overhead as Gina and I hurried to the car. I helped her into the backseat and made quick introductions before running around to the driver's side.

"Well?" Kyra asked as I started the engine.

"He's already gone," I said.

"Audition in Midland," Gina added. "He left about fifteen minutes ago.

"Gina says there's only one road that would have lots of cars on it like you saw," I explained. "State Route thirty-three."

Kyra thought for a second and nodded. "Yes! I remember seeing a mile marker."

"Where? What number?"

She shook her head. "I didn't see the numbers, only the shape."

In the backseat, Gina growled. "What are you waiting for? Go!"

My mind was at war as I drove across town. Just touching the steering wheel made my palms sweat and my muscles twitch. Driving with Kyra and Gina in the car was much harder than when it was just me. Any moment, another car could come hurtling through an intersection like before and in an instant, I could lose my sister and my friend the way I had lost my mom. I wanted to drive slow, cautious, watching for every possible collision. But Jake was out there, and I had to warn him.

Kyra and Gina navigated for me since they both knew the streets better than I did. Soon we had reached the entrance to the highway. Another wave of ice and nausea washed over me when I saw the cars whipping by.

"You can do it," Kyra urged. "Just merge in. You've got it."

I must have looked like an old grandma at the wheel, the way I was gripping it so tightly—at ten and two—leaning forward in my seat, staring over the top of it, but I couldn't help it. By then, the rain beat down on the windshield so hard that even with the wipers going full speed, sheets of water cascaded across the glass and warped what I could see of the road. It made the lines waver and cast red halos around the taillights of the cars ahead. Outside the glow of my headlights, darkness swallowed the rest of the world. All that remained was the rain, the highway, and somewhere ahead, Jake on his motorcycle, unaware.

"Faster." Gina shook my shoulder. "You're never going to catch him like this."

I stepped on the gas, strangling the steering wheel and trying to ignore the sharp edges of panic that lodged in my chest. Overhead, lightning tore open the sky, throwing everything into a photo negative for an instant. I blinked, spots dancing before my eyes.

"Watch out!" Kyra screamed.

The car ahead had slowed and I swerved out of the way just in time to avoid rear-ending it. I pumped the brakes the way I had been taught in driver's ed, but still we skidded, the back end fishtailing before I gained control again. I think I screamed. Or maybe it was Kyra. Or Gina. Or all of us. My ears rang and my heart felt like it was lodged in my throat.

Ahead, the freeway glowed red, brake lights flashing like a monochromatic Christmas tree. Traffic slowed to the point that we were practically crawling. Another flash of lightning lit the scene and then vanished again, followed this time by a rolling growl of thunder.

"Oh, no," Kyra said.

I could barely ask, "What is it?"

She just stared at me, her face ghostly pale in the glow of the dashboard lights.

But I didn't need her to tell me. Now I could see for myself. The road flares. The highway patrolman in his long, dark raincoat, the reflective tape across his chest and sleeves glowing in the beam of the headlights as he waived traffic to the left-hand lane.

We were too late.

I didn't cry. Not on the outside, anyway. Inside I was screaming so hard it felt like my lungs had been ripped out. Why Jake? Why now? Why did Kyra and I have to see these things that were going to happen if we couldn't do anything to stop them? Why? Why? *Why?*

We crawled along in the traffic, rain pouring down like misery. I could see the wreck ahead. Not one car, but several. Twisted, mangled, broken. I thought of Jake on his motorcycle with no seat belt to hold him back, no metal protection around his body, and I wanted to scream again. We passed the wreckage in slow motion, Kyra, Gina, and I silent, staring straight ahead. The only sound in the car was the beating of the rain on the roof and the steady *thwap, thwap, thwap* of the windshield wipers. As soon as we passed the pileup, I swerved between the flares into the vacant right lane and threw the car into park.

Kyra grabbed my sleeve. "What are you doing? It's over!"

I pulled my arm away and pushed the car door open. "Stay with Gina!" I yelled, and ran out into the rain.

My eyes flutter open but for a moment I can't see anything—only white. The air bag. I want to hit it away but it hurts to move. All I can do is to turn my head—slowly—to the side, and even that is painful.

Mom is leaning back against the passenger seat and her eyes are closed. It almost looks as if she's sleeping, except that her mouth hangs open and the sound coming out of it is like an animal's whimper.

I try to draw in a breath to call her name, but my chest feels heavy and full of knives. I can only take the smallest of gasps. Instead, I inch my hand over to where hers lies motionless on her knee and her fingers close around mine.

Faces appear in the space left by the shattered window and then move away. I can't focus on any of them as the bright red lights pirouette through the scene.

Hands reach in through my door. I can feel the air bag deflate; the seat move; pressure on my neck, my back.

"She'll need a board," a man's voice says.

A woman reaches in through the passenger window and presses her fingers against my mom's neck. She's wearing light blue rubber gloves. They come away red. She turns around and yells, "We need to get this door open, stat!" then back to my mom, "Stay with us, sweetheart. Help is on the way." She lifts one of Mom's eyelids and shines a bright light into it. "Fixed and dilated. Damn!"

Another sound comes from my mom's throat, like air leaking from a tire. Her grip on my hand tightens and then goes slack.

"Mom!" I cry, but the only sound I can make is a whisper.

The rain instantly soaked through my clothes and plastered my hair to my cheeks. I slammed the door behind me and ran.

"Miss!" an officer called. "Stop right there!"

But I couldn't stop. Not until I knew.

My legs felt like they had been filled with wet sand. Water streamed into my eyes faster than I could blink it away. The officer yelled after me, but it only made me run faster.

As I neared the wreckage, the scene took on a surreal edge. Several people clustered at the side of the road, some moving, some not. I passed a shirtless man holding a wad of cloth to his head. Another sitting on the asphalt, cradling his arm. The wheel on an overturned car spinning in lazy circles. Men in yellow prying open a door of another with what looked like a giant claw. Red and white lights chasing each other across the wreckage. A highway patrol car up ahead, parked at an angle across the road.

At least four cars were piled on top of each other, mashed together so completely that I couldn't even see a trace of Jake's Indian.

I knew I was crying then, tears hot on my cheeks and mixing with the cool rain. "Jake!" I screamed. "Jake!"

"Miss! Back away from—"

Just then, lightning flashed again so bright that it must have been directly overhead. Its sharp, electric smell cut through the wet odor of burned rubber and gasoline. Thunder followed instantaneously, the concussion like a pair of hands clapped over my ears. Shock waves trembled through the ground beneath my feet.

I crouched instinctively and threw my hands over my head. I couldn't see. I couldn't hear. I could barely think. I just wanted to die right there so the pain would stop.

That's when I heard his voice in the distance calling my name. I closed my eyes, waiting for the white light. Wishing to go with him and never return.

"Ashlyn?"

My eyes flew open.

"Ashlyn!"

It was him! I stood shakily, afraid to move too quickly and end the dream.

Jake ran toward me, whole, beautiful, alive. He caught me in his arms and lifted me off the ground. "Are you crazy? What are you doing here?"

I grabbed fistfuls of his shirt, held him to me. "I thought you were dead," I sobbed. "I tried to stop you, but . . . but . . ."

He set me on my feet again, searching my face. "I pulled

over," he said. "When you kept calling my cell, I figured it must be urgent, but by the time I could answer it, the reception went out."

"The storm," I said.

"Must be. I was just about to pull back onto the road when a car came skidding past me sideways. It happened so fast I don't even know . . ." He shook his head, remembering. "That car hit the one in front of it, and then the one behind couldn't stop fast enough and . . ." He looked over at the pile of twisted metal and glass.

I held him tight again. I didn't need to hear any more. I knew; I had seen what could have happened to him.

He wrapped me in his arms, resting his chin on top of my head. For the first time in a very long while, I knew where I belonged.

EPILOGUE

Jake holds tight to my hand as we walk through the brightly lit halls of the hospital. I hold tight to Kyra's hand. Gina's in room 327. I keep repeating the number in my head. *Three twenty-seven. Three twenty-seven.* Otherwise, my mind would drift back to another night, another trip down the sterile hallway. *The paramedic and the ER nurse bending over me. The blur of lights overhead. Cool hands in latex gloves checking my respiration, my pulse. Stone faces and exchanged glances when I ask about my mom.*

The barrage of sensations around me are uncomfortably familiar—the strange mixed scent of cafeteria food, flowers, and antiseptic; the squeak of gurney wheels rolling over polished floors; the soft ding of the elevator chime. But instead of green scrubs and powder blue gloves, the nurses in this hallway wear bright prints and wide smiles. The cries we hear from the rooms we pass are not cries of pain or loss; they are energetic cries, demanding cries, new-life cries.

Outside Gina's door, we pause until she calls out to us impatiently. "Get in here."

Single file we shuffle into the room.

Gina's sitting up in the bed, a pink little bundle in her arms. "Come on over," she says softly. "Talia wants to meet you."

Talia Lyn came into the world on Route 33 at exactly 9:57 P.M. One of the paramedics from the accident scene helped to deliver her in the backseat of my car. The television news crews who had gathered to film the drama of the accident quickly dubbed Talia the miracle baby, even though she hadn't actually been part of the pileup. She is unimpressed by the attention, and sleeps peacefully in her mother's arms.

"What do you think?" Gina asks. "Not bad, huh?"

"Not bad at all." Jake gently rubs his thumb over Talia's downy black hair, and his face fills with wonder.

"It's a pretty name," Kyra says.

"Thanks." Gina smiles sheepishly. "It was supposed to be Natalia, but when I ran the numbers, the vibration was all wrong."

I can't help but laugh. Jake squeezes my hand tighter and I smile up at him. We might not have been able to change the past, but we had changed the power it held over us. I don't know what the future holds—I don't want to know—but we had changed the here, the now, and that is enough.

Kyra and I haven't had another trance since the night of the accident. We can only guess why. It's like we crossed some sort of threshold by stopping what we saw. It's been four weeks and not a ripple.

Kyra is moving home today. Dad seems happy to have her coming back . . . at least he's smiling more. He's also a little more relaxed. He still spends a lot of time in his office, though. I suppose he isn't ready yet to take on the chaos outside his office door. That's okay. Like Gina said, everyone deals with grief in their own way. He'll come around. Eventually.

Michelle calls while I'm helping Kyra to move her things back into our room.

"I haven't seen you for eons," she says. "Do you want to go do something?"

I glance at Kyra and she mouths, "Just go."

"Jake's playing with a band over in Westerville tonight," I tell Michelle. "I was thinking of going. You want to come?"

She practically squeals her approval. "Sounds perfect. What time should I pick you up?"

"That's okay," I tell her. "I'll drive."

***

Michelle and I are sitting at a front table at the Ice House, where Jake's band is about to go on. Michelle's eyes keep straying as we're talking and I turn around to see Trey at a table behind us.

"Go on," I say.

She hesitates for only a moment and then gives me a quick hug. "I knew you'd understand," she whispers, and runs off to join him.

For an instant, I feel a strange tug in my stomach as I remember the last time she said that to me. A lot has happened since then. But I don't dwell on that like I used to. I can't. The past is past. It can't be changed. I've learned to accept that.

When Jake's band comes onstage, I pull out my old Nikon. When I set up the shots, I still look for the small things, the textures, the details, but for the first time, I also take pictures of the whole. I don't feel the need to break it up anymore.

The band is just okay, but Jake is phenomenal. He looks more content and relaxed than I've ever seen him before. I'm thinking he must really love music if it makes him so happy, and then his eyes meet mine. That's when I understand it's not just about the music.

Kyra's sitting on her bed reading when I come home. She glances up when I walk in the room. "How was it?"

I can feel the smile building all the way up from my

toenails. "Perfect." I sit at the desk and pull off my shoes and socks. "Jake was fantastic. I wish you would have come with us."

She just smiles and shakes her head. People and crowds are still not her thing. "Your boss lady called at least three times while you were gone. She wants to make sure you're going to be there in the morning."

"I'll be there."

I was finally able to convince Dad to let me go back to work at ShutterBugz after Gina had the baby and Carole was left seriously shorthanded. It's not quite the same, though, now that Jake has quit working for his uncle. I'll probably only stay there until she can find someone else to take my place. Knowing Carole, that may be a while.

I take off my earrings and lay them on the desk. I'm just reaching back to unclasp my necklace when I find myself scratching at a familiar itch. My eyes go wide and I clamp a hand to the back of my neck.

"Ashlyn?" Kyra's voice sounds far away.

I feel my fingers close around a pencil.

And then everything goes black.